MESSAGE FROM VALDEZ

Valdez dismounted and went to his knees over the man, raising his arm gently to look at the wound. The shotgun charge had torn through his side at the waist, ripping away his belt and part of his shirt and leather chaps.

"You should have this taken care of," Valdez said. "You know somebody can sew you up?"

The Mexican's eyes were glazed, wet looking. "What do you put in that thing?"

"I told you, something for rabbits. Listen, I'm going to get your horse and put you on it."

"I can't ride anywhere."

"Sure you can." Valdez lowered the Mexican's arm and gave his shoulder a pat. The Mexican winced and Valdez smiled. "You ride to Mr. Tanner, all right? Tell him Valdez is coming. You hear what I said? Valdez is coming. But listen, friend, I think you better go there quick."

*Other Exciting Westerns by Elmore Leonard
Available from Dell*

THE BOUNTY HUNTERS

VALDEZ IS COMING

Elmore Leonard

A DELL BOOK

Published by
Dell Publishing
a division of
Bantam Doubleday Dell Publishing Group, Inc.
1540 Broadway
New York, New York 10036

Copyright © 1970 by Elmore Leonard

ISBN: 0-440-21307-X

Printed in the United States of America

Published simultaneously in Canada

August 1993

10 9 8 7 6 5 4 3 2 1

RAD

ONE

●

Picture the ground rising on the east side of the pasture with scrub trees thick on the slope and pines higher up. This is where everybody was. Not all in one place but scattered in small groups, about a dozen men in the scrub, the front line, the shooters who couldn't just stand around. They'd fire at the shack when they felt like it, or when Mr. Tanner passed the word, they would all fire at once.

Others were up in the pines and on the road that ran along the crest of the hill, some three hundred yards from the shack across the pasture. Those watching made bets whether the man in the shack would give himself up or get shot first.

It was Saturday and that's why everybody had the time. They would arrive in Lanoria, hear about what happened, and shortly after, head out to the cattle company pasture. Most of the men went out alone, leaving their families in town, though there were a few women who came. The other women waited. And the people who had business in town and couldn't leave waited. Now and then a few would come back from the pasture to have a drink or their dinner and would tell what was going on. No, they hadn't got him yet. Still inside the line shack and not showing his face. But they'd get him. A few more would go out from town when they heard this. Also a wagon from De Spain's went out with whiskey. That's how the saloon was set up in the pines overlooking the pasture. Somebody said it was like the goddam Fourth of July.

Barely a mile from town those going out would hear the gunfire—like a skirmish way over the other side of the woods, thin specks of sound—and this would hurry them. They were careful though, topping the slope, looking across the pasture, getting their bearings, then peering around to see who was there. They would see a friend and ask about this Mr. Tanner, and the friend would point him out.

The man there in the dark suit: thin and bony, not big especially, but looking like he was made of gristle and hard to kill, with a moustache and a thin nose and a dark dusty hat worn over his eyes. That was him. They had heard about Frank Tanner, but not many had ever seen him. He had a place south in the foothills of the Santa Ritas and almost to the border. They said he had an army riding for him, Americans and Mexicans, and that his place was like a barracks except for the women. They said he traded horses and cattle and guns across into Mexico to the revolutionary forces and he had all the riders in case the Federales came down on him; also in case his customers ever decided not to pay. Sure he had at least twenty-five men and he didn't graze a head of beef himself. Where were they? somebody wanted to know. Driving a herd south. That's what he had come here for, cattle; bought them from Maricopa.

Somebody else said he had brought his wife along—"God*dam*, a good-looking young woman, I'll tell you, some years younger than he is"—and she was waiting for him at the Republic Hotel right now, staying up in his room, and not many people had seen her.

They would look at Mr. Tanner, then across the cattle pasture to the line shack three hundred yards away. It was a little bake-oven of a hut, wood framed and made of sod and built against a rise where there were pines so the hut would be in shade part of the day. There were no windows in the hut, no gear lying around to show anybody lived there. The hut stood in the sun now with its door closed, the door chipped and splintered by all the bullets that had poured into it and through it.

Off to the right where the pine shapes against the sky rounded and became willows, there in the trees by the creek bed, was the man's wagon and team. In the wagon were the supplies he'd bought that morning in Lanoria before Mr. Tanner spotted him.

Out in front of the hut about ten or fifteen feet there was something on the ground. From the slope three hundred yards away nobody could tell what it was until a man came who had field glasses. He looked up and said, frowning, it was a doll: one made of cloth scraps, a stuffed doll with buttons for eyes.

"The woman must have dropped it," somebody said.

"The *woman?*" the man with the field glasses said.

A Lipan Apache woman who was his wife or his woman or just with him. Mr. Tanner hadn't been clear about that. All they knew was that there was a woman in the hut with him and if the man wanted her to stay and get shot that was his business.

A Mr. Beaudry, the government land agent for the county, was there. Also Mr. Malson, manager of the Maricopa Cattle Company, and a horsebreaker by the name of Diego Luz, who was big for a Mexican but never offensive and who drank pretty well.

Mr. Beaudry, nodding and also squinting so he could picture the man inside the line shack, said, "There was something peculiar about him. I mean having a name like Orlando Rincón."

"He worked for me," Mr. Malson said. He was looking at Mr. Tanner. "I mistrusted him and I believe that was part of it, his name being Orlando Rincón."

"Johnson," Mr. Tanner said.

"I hired him two, three times," Mr. Malson said. "For heavy work. When I had work you couldn't pay a white man to do."

"His name is Johnson," Mr. Tanner said. "There is no fuzzhead by the name of Orlando Rincón. I'm telling you this fuzzhead is from the Fort Hauchuca Tenth fuzzhead Cavalry and his name was Johnson when he killed James C. Erin six months ago and nothing else."

He spoke as you might speak to young children to press something into their minds. This man seemed to have no feeling and he never smiled, but there was no reason to doubt him.

* * *

Bob Valdez arrived at the Maricopa pasture about noon. He was riding shotgun on the Hatch and Hodges run from St. David. He swung down from the boot, holding his sawed-off shotgun in the air, as the stage edged past the whiskey wagon.

Somebody standing at the tailgate with a glass in his hand said, "Hey, here's the town constable," and those nearby looked toward Bob Valdez in his dark suit and buttoned-up shirt, wearing a collar button but no tie or bandana; Valdez with his hat straight and slightly forward, the brim flat and the low crown undented.

"We'll get that nigger out of there now," somebody said, and a couple of others gave a little laugh to show they knew the person who said it was kidding.

Bob Valdez smiled, going along with it, though not knowing what they meant. "Out of where?" he said.

They explained it to him and he nodded, listening, his gaze moving over the shooters in the scrub, out to the line shack across the pasture and back to the slope, to the group of men a little way down from him. He saw Mr. Beaudry and Mr. Malson and Diego Luz, and the one they said was Mr. Tanner, there, talking to an R. L. Davis, who rode for Maricopa when he was working.

Bob Valdez watched the two men, both of them cut from the same stringy hide and looking like father and son: Mr. Tanner talking, never smiling, barely moving his mouth; R. L. Davis standing hip-cocked, posing with his revolver and rifle and a cartridge belt hanging over one shoulder, and the funneled, pointed brim of his sweaty hat nodding up and down as he listened to Mr. Tanner, grinning at what Mr. Tanner said, laughing out loud while Mr. Tanner did not show the twitch of a lip. Bob Valdez did not like R. L. Davis or any of the R. L. Davises in the world. He was civil, he listened to them, but God, there were a lot of them to listen to.

Well, all right, Bob Valdez thought. He walked down the slope to the group of men, nodding to Mr. Beaudry and Mr. Malson as they looked up. He waited a moment, not looking directly at Tanner, waiting for one of them to introduce him. Finally he held out his hand. "I'm Bob Valdez," he said, smiling a little.

Mr. Tanner looked at him, but did not shake hands. His gaze shifted as Mr. Malson said, "Bob's a town constable. He works a few nights a week in the Mexican part of town."

"The nights I'm here," Bob Valdez said. "Not on a stage run. See, I work for Hatch and Hodges too."

This time Mr. Tanner turned to say something to R. L. Davis, a couple of words that could have been about anything, and R. L. Davis laughed. Bob Valdez was a grown man; he was forty years old and as big as Mr. Tanner, but he stood there and didn't know what to do. He gripped the shotgun and was glad he had something to hold on to. He would have to stay near Mr. Tanner because he was the center of what was going on here. Soon they would discuss the situation and decide what to do. As the law-enforcement man he, Bob Valdez, should be in on the discussion and the decision. Of course. If someone was going to arrest Orlando Rincón or Johnson or whatever his name was, then he should be the one to do it; he was a town constable. They were out of town maybe, but where did the town end? The town had moved out here now; it was the same thing.

He could wait for Rincón to give up. Then arrest him.

If he wasn't dead already.

"Mr. Malson." Bob Valdez stepped toward the cattle company manager, who glanced over but looked out across the pasture again, indifferent.

"I wondered if maybe he's already dead," Valdez said.

Mr. Malson said, "Why don't you find out?"

"I was thinking," Valdez said, "if he was dead we could stand here a long time."

R. L. Davis adjusted his hat, which he did often, grabbing the funneled brim, loosening it on his head and pulling it down close to his eyes again and shifting from one cocked hip to the other. "Valdez here's got better things to do," R. L. Davis said. "He's busy."

"No," Bob Valdez said. "I was thinking of the one inside there, Rincón. He's dead or he's alive. He's alive, maybe he wants to give himself up. In there he has time to think, uh? Maybe——" He stopped. Not one of them was listening. Not even R. L. Davis.

Mr. Malson was looking at the whiskey wagon; it was on the road above them and over a little ways, with men standing by it being served off the tailgate. "I think we could use something," Mr. Malson said. His gaze went to Diego Luz the horsebreaker and Diego straightened up; not much, but a little. He was heavy and very dark and his shirt was tight across the thickness of his body. They said that Diego Luz hit green horses on the muzzle with his fist and they minded him. He had the hands for it; they hung at his sides, not touching or fooling with anything. They turned open, gestured when Mr. Malson told him to get the whiskey, and as he moved off climbing the slope, one hand held his holstered revolver to his leg.

Mr. Malson looked up at the sky, squinting and taking his hat off and putting it on again. He took off his coat and held it hooked over his shoulder by one finger, said something, gestured, and he and Mr. Beaudry and Mr. Tanner moved a few yards down the slope to a hollow where there was good shade. It was about two or two thirty then, hot, fairly still and quiet considering the number of people there. Only some of them in the pines and down in the scrub could be seen from where Bob Valdez stood wondering whether he should follow the three men down to the hollow or wait for Diego Luz, who was at the whiskey wagon now where most of the sounds that carried came from: a voice, a word or two that was suddenly clear, or laughter, and people would look up to see what was going on. Some of them by the whiskey wagon had lost interest in the line shack. Others were still watching though: those farther along the road sitting in wagons and buggies. This was a day people would remember and talk about. "Sure, I was there," the man in the buggy would be saying a year from now in a saloon over in Benson or St. David or somewhere. "The day they got that Army deserter, he had a Big-Fifty Sharps and an old dragoon pistol, and I'll tell you it was ticklish business."

Down in that worn-out pasture, dusty and spotted with desert growth, prickly pear and brittlebush, there was just the sun. It showed the ground clearly all the way to just in front of the line shack where now, toward midafternoon, there was shadow coming out from the trees and from the mound the hut was set against.

Somebody in the scrub must have seen the door open. The shout came from there, and Bob Valdez and everybody on the slope were looking by the time the Lipan Apache woman had reached the edge of the shade. She walked out from the hut toward the willow trees carrying a bucket, not hurrying or even looking toward the slope.

Nobody fired at her, though this was not so strange. Putting the front sight on a sod hut and on a person are two different things. The men in the scrub and in the pines didn't know this woman. They weren't after her. She had just appeared. There she was; and no one was sure what to do about her.

She was in the trees by the creek awhile, then she was in the open again, walking back toward the hut with the bucket and not hurrying at all, a small figure way across the pasture almost without shape or color, with only the long skirt reaching to the ground to tell it was the woman.

So he's alive, Bob Valdez thought. And he wants to stay alive and he's not giving himself up.

He thought about the woman's nerve and whether Orlando Rincón had sent her out or she had decided this herself. You couldn't tell about an Indian woman. Maybe this was expected of her. The woman didn't count; the man did. You could lose the woman and get another one.

Mr. Tanner didn't look at R. L. Davis. His gaze held on the Lipan Apache woman, inched along with her toward the hut; but he must have known R. L. Davis was right next to him.

"She's saying she don't give a goddam about you and your rifle," Mr. Tanner said.

R. L. Davis looked at him funny. Then he said, "Shoot her?" like he hoped that's what Mr. Tanner meant.

"You could make her jump some," Mr. Tanner said.

Now R. L. Davis was on stage and he knew it, and Bob Valdez could tell he knew it by the way he levered the Winchester, raised it, and fired all in one motion, and as the dust kicked behind the Indian woman, who kept walking and didn't look up, R. L. Davis fired and fired and fired as fast as he could lever and half aim and with everybody watching him, hurrying him, he put four good ones right behind the woman. His last bullet socked into the door just as she reached it, and now she did pause and look up at the slope, staring up like she was waiting for him to fire again and giving him a good target if he wanted it.

Mr. Beaudry laughed out loud. "She don't give a goddam about your rifle."

It stung R. L. Davis, which it was intended to do.

"I wasn't aiming at her."

"But she doesn't know that." Mr. Beaudry was grinning, twisting his moustache, turning then and reaching out a hand as Diego Luz approached them with the whiskey.

"Hell, I wanted to hit her she'd be laying there, you know it."

"Well now, you tell her that," Mr. Beaudry said, working the cork loose, "and she'll know it." He took a drink from the bottle and passed it to Mr. Malson, who offered the bottle to Mr. Tanner, who shook his head. Mr. Malson took a drink and saw R. L. Davis staring at him, so he handed the bottle to him. R. L. Davis jerked the bottle up, took a long swallow and that part was over.

Mr. Malson said to Mr. Tanner, "You don't want any?"

"Not right now," Mr. Tanner answered. He continued to stare out across the pasture.

Mr. Malson watched him. "You feel strongly about this Army deserter."

"I told you," Mr. Tanner said, "he killed a man was a friend of mine."

"No, I don't believe you did."

"James C. Erin, sutler at Fort Huachuca," Mr. Tanner said. "He came across a tulapai still this nigger soldier was working with some Indians. The nigger thought Erin would tell the Army people, so he shot him and ran off with a woman."

"And you saw him this morning."

"I had come in last night to see this gentleman," Mr. Tanner said, nodding toward Malson. "This morning I was getting ready to leave when I saw him, him and the woman."

"I was right there," R. L. Davis said. "Right, Mr. Tanner? Him and I was on the porch by the Republic Hotel and Rincón goes by in the wagon. Mr. Tanner said, 'You know that man?' I said, 'Only that he's lived up north of town a few months. Him and his woman.'

'Well, I know him,' Mr. Tanner said. 'That man's an Army deserter wanted for murder.' I said, 'Well let's go get him.' He had a start on us and that's how he got to the hut before we could grab on to him. He's been holed up ever since.''

Mr. Malson said, ''Then you didn't talk to him.''

''Listen,'' Mr. Tanner said, ''I've kept that man's face before my eyes this past year.''

Bob Valdez, somewhat behind Mr. Tanner and to the side, moved in a little closer. ''You know this is the same man?''

Mr. Tanner looked around. He stared at Valdez. That's all he did, just stared.

''I mean, we have to be sure,'' Bob Valdez said. ''It's a serious thing.''

Now Mr. Malson and Mr. Beaudry were looking up at him. ''We,'' Mr. Beaudry said. ''I'll tell you what, Roberto. We need help we'll call you. All right?''

''You hired me,'' Bob Valdez said, standing alone above them. He was serious, but he shrugged and smiled a little to take the edge off the words. ''What did you hire me for?''

''Well,'' Mr. Beaudry said, acting it out, looking up past Bob Valdez and along the road both ways. ''I was to see some drunk Mexicans, I'd point them out.''

After that, for a while, the men with the whiskey bottle forgot Bob Valdez. They stayed in the shade of the hollow watching the line shack, waiting for the Army deserter to realize it was all over for him. He would realize it and open the door and be cut down as he came outside. It was a matter of time only.

Bob Valdez stayed on the open part of the slope that

was turning to shade, sitting now like an Apache with a suit on and every once in a while making a cigarette and smoking it slowly and thinking about himself and Mr. Tanner and the others, then thinking about the Army deserter, then thinking about himself again.

He didn't have to stay here. He didn't have to be a town constable. He didn't have to work for the stage company. He didn't have to listen to Mr. Beaudry and Mr. Malson and smile when they said those things. He didn't have a wife or any kids. He didn't have land that he owned. He could go anywhere he wanted.

Diego Luz was coming over. Diego Luz had a wife and a daughter almost grown and some little kids and he had to stay, sure.

Diego Luz squatted next to him, his arms on his knees and his big hands that he used for breaking horses hanging in front of him.

"Stay near if they want you for something," Bob Valdez said. He was watching Beaudry tilt the bottle up. Diego Luz said nothing.

"One of them bends over," Bob Valdez said then, "you kiss it, uh?"

Diego Luz looked at him, patient about it. Not angry or stirred. "Why don't you go home?"

"He says get me a bottle, you run."

"I get it. I don't run."

"Smile and hold your hat, uh?"

"And don't talk so much."

"Not unless they talk to you first."

"You better go home," Diego said.

Bob Valdez said, "That's why you hit the horses."

"Listen," Diego Luz said. "They pay me to break

horses. They pay you to talk to drunks and keep them from killing somebody. They don't pay you for what you think or how you feel. So if you take their money keep your mouth shut. All right?"

Bob Valdez smiled. "I'm kidding you."

Diego Luz got up and walked away, down toward the hollow. The hell with him, he was thinking. Maybe he was kidding, but the hell with him. He was also thinking that maybe he could get a drink from that bottle. Maybe there would be a half inch left nobody wanted and Mr. Malson would tell him to kill it.

But it was already finished. R. L. Davis was playing with the bottle, holding it by the neck and flipping it up and catching it as it came down. Beaudry was saying, "What about after dark?" And looking at Mr. Tanner, who was thinking about something else and didn't notice.

R. L. Davis stopped flipping the bottle. He said, "Put some men on the rise right above the hut; he comes out, bust him."

"Well, they should get the men over there," Mr. Beaudry said, looking at the sky. "It won't be long till dark."

"Where's he going?" Mr. Malson said.

The others looked up, stopped in whatever they were doing or thinking by the suddenness of Mr. Malson's voice.

"Hey, Valdez!" R. L. Davis yelled out. "Where you think you're going?"

Bob Valdez had circled them and was already below them on the slope, leaving the pines now and entering the scrub brush. He didn't stop or look back.

"Valdez!"

Mr. Tanner raised one hand to silence R. L. Davis, all the time watching Bob Valdez getting smaller, going straight through the scrub, not just walking or passing the time but going right out to the pasture.

"Look at him," Mr. Malson said. There was some admiration in his voice.

"He's dumber than he looks," R. L. Davis said, then jumped a little as Mr. Tanner touched his arm.

"Come on," Mr. Tanner said. "With the rifle." And he started down the slope, hurrying and not seeming to care if he might stumble on the loose gravel.

Bob Valdez was now halfway across the pasture, the shotgun pointed down at his side, his eyes not leaving the door of the line shack. The door was probably already open enough for a rifle barrel to poke through. He guessed the Army deserter was covering him, letting him get as close as he wanted; the closer he came the easier to hit him.

Now he could see all the bullet marks in the door and the clean inner wood where the door was splintered. Two people in that little bake-oven of a place. He saw the door move.

He saw the rag doll on the ground. It was a strange thing, the woman having a doll. Valdez hardly glanced at it but was aware of the button eyes looking up and the discomforted twist of the red wool mouth. Then, just past the doll, when he was wondering if he would go right up to the door and knock on it and wouldn't that be a crazy thing, like visiting somebody, the door opened and the Negro was in the doorway filling it, standing there in pants and boots but without a shirt in that hot place, and holding a long-barreled dragoon that was already cocked.

They stood twelve feet apart looking at each other, close enough so that no one could fire from the slope.

"I can kill you first," the Negro said, "if you raise it."

With his free hand, the left one, Bob Valdez motioned back over his shoulder. "There's a man there said you killed somebody a year ago."

"What man?"

"Said his name is Tanner."

The Negro shook his head, once each way.

"Said your name is Johnson."

"You know my name."

"I'm telling you what he said."

"Where'd I kill this man?"

"Huachuca."

The Negro hesitated. "That was some time ago I was in the Tenth. More than a year."

"You a deserter?"

"I served it out."

"Then you got something that says so."

"In the wagon, there's a bag there my things are in."

"Will you talk to this man Tanner?"

"If I can hold from busting him."

"Listen, why did you run this morning?"

"They come chasing. I don't know what they want." He lowered the gun a little, his brown-stained tired-looking eyes staring intently at Bob Valdez. "What would you do? They come on the run. Next thing I know they firing at us."

"Will you go with me and talk to him?"

The Negro hesitated again. Then shook his head. "I don't know him."

"Then he won't know you."

"He didn't know me this morning."

"All right," Bob Valdez said. "I'll get your paper says you were discharged. Then we'll show it to this man, uh?"

The Negro thought it over before he nodded, very slowly, as if still thinking. "All right. Bring him here, I'll say a few words to him."

Bob Valdez smiled a little. "You can point that gun some other way."

"Well . . ." the Negro said, "if everybody's friends." He lowered the revolver to his side.

The wagon was in the willow trees by the creek. Off to the right. But Bob Valdez did not turn right away in that direction. He backed away, watching Orlando Rincón for no reason that he knew of. Maybe because the man was holding a gun and that was reason enough.

He had backed off six or seven feet when Orlando Rincón shoved the revolver down into his belt. Bob Valdez turned and started for the trees.

It was at this moment that he looked across the pasture. He saw Mr. Tanner and R. L. Davis at the edge of the scrub trees but wasn't sure it was them. Something tried to tell him it was them, but he did not accept it until he was off to the right, out of the line of fire, and by then the time to yell at them or run toward them was past. R. L. Davis had the Winchester up and was firing.

They say R. L. Davis was drunk or he would have

pinned him square. As it was, the bullet shaved Rincón and plowed past him into the hut.

Bob Valdez saw Rincón half turn and he saw Rincón's accusing eyes as Rincón pulled the long-barreled dragoon from his belt.

"They weren't supposed to," Bob Valdez said, holding one hand out as if to stop Rincón. "Listen, they weren't supposed to do that!"

The revolver was free, and Rincón was cocking it. "Don't!" Bob Valdez said. "Don't do it!" Looking right into the Negro's eyes and seeing it was no use, that Rincón was going to shoot him, and suddenly hurrying, he jerked the shotgun up and pulled both triggers so that the explosions came out in one blast and Orlando Rincón was spun and thrown back inside.

They came out across the pasture to have a look, some going inside where they found the woman and brought her out, everybody noticing she would have a child in about a month. Those by the doorway made room as Mr. Tanner and R. L. Davis approached.

Diego Luz came over by Bob Valdez, who had not moved. Valdez stood watching them and he saw Mr. Tanner look down at Rincón and after a moment shake his head.

"It looked like him," Mr. Tanner said. "It sure looked like him."

He saw R. L. Davis squint at Mr. Tanner. "It ain't the one you said?"

Mr. Tanner shook his head again. "I've seen him before though. I know I've seen him somewheres."

Bob Valdez saw R. L. Davis shrug. "You ask me, they all look alike." He was yawning then, fooling with his hat, and then his eyes swiveled over to Bob Valdez standing with the empty shotgun.

"Constable," R. L. Davis said. "You went and killed the wrong coon."

Bob Valdez started for him, raising the shotgun to swing it like a club, but Diego Luz caught him from behind and locked a big arm around his neck, under his chin, until he was still and Mr. Tanner and the others had moved off.

TWO

●

A man can be in two different places and he will be two different men. Maybe if you think of more places he will be more men, but two is enough for now. This is Bob Valdez washing his hands in the creek and resting in the willows after digging the hole and lowering Orlando Rincón into it and covering him with dirt and stones, resting and watching the Lipan Apache woman who sat in silence by the grave of the man whose child she would have in a month.

This is one Bob Valdez. The forty-year-old town constable and stage-line shotgun rider. A good, hardworking man. And hard looking, with a dark hard face that was creased and leathery; but don't go by looks, they said, Bob Valdez was kindly and respectful. One of the good ones. The whores in Inez's place on Commercial Street would call to him from their windows; even the white-skinned girls who had come from St. Louis, they liked him too. Bob Valdez would wave at them and sometimes he would go in and after being with the girl would have a cup of coffee with Inez. They had known each other when they were children in Tucson. That was all right, going to Inez's place. Mr. Beaudry and Mr. Malson and the others could try to think of a time when Bob Valdez might have drunk too much or swaggered or had a certain smart-aleck look on his face, but they would never recall such a time. Yes, this Bob Valdez was all right.

Another Bob Valdez inside the Bob Valdez in the willows that evening had worked for the Army at one time and had been a contract guide when General Crook chased Geronimo down into the Madres. He was a tracker out of Whipple Barracks first, then out of Fort Thomas, then in charge of the Apache police at Whiteriver. He would sit at night eating with them and talking with them as he learned the Chiricahua dialect. He would keep up with them all day and shoot his Springfield carbine one hell of a lot better than any of them could shoot. He had taken scalps but never showed them to anyone and had thrown them away by the time Geronimo was in Oklahoma and he had gone to work for the stage company, Hatch and Hodges, to live as a civilized man. Shortly after that he was named town constable in Lanoria at twenty-five dollars a month, getting the job because he got along with people, including the Mexicans in town who drank too much on Saturday night, and this was the Bob Valdez that Mr. Beaudry and Mr. Malson and the others knew. They had never met the first Bob Valdez.

And they had forgotten about the second Bob Valdez; they had gone, everyone cleared out of the Maricopa pasture. He was alone with the Lipan

Apache woman as evening settled and the grove in the willow trees became dark.

He had not spoken to the woman. He had touched her shoulder before digging the grave—when she had tried to take the shovel from him to do it herself—he had touched her, easing her to the ground, and she had sat unmoving while he formed the hole and dug deep into the soil. He would look at her and smile, but her expression gave him nothing in return. She wasn't an attractive woman. She was a round shape in a dirty gray dress with yellow strands of beads. He did not know how old she was. She was something sitting there watching him but not watching him. She would build a fire and sit here all night and in the morning she would probably be gone.

He had never seen the woman before. He had seen Orlando Rincón in Lanoria. He had recognized him, but had never spoken to him before today. Rincón had a one-loop spread a half day's ride south of Lanoria that he and the woman tended alone. That much was all Bob Valdez knew about them. They had come into town for something and now the man was dead and the woman was alone with her unborn child. Like that, her life, whatever it had been before, good or bad, was gone.

He watched the woman rise from the grave to water the wagon horses in the creek. She returned and made a fire, lighting it with a match. Valdez went over to her then, fashioning a cigarette and leaning in to light it in the fire, taking his time because he wasn't sure of the words he wanted to use.

In Spanish he said, "Where will you go?" and repeated it in the Chiricahua dialect when she continued to stare at him, and now she pointed off beyond the creek.

"This should not have happened," he said. "Your husband had done nothing. It was a mistake." He leaned closer to see her clearly in the firelight. "I did it to him, but I didn't want to. He didn't understand and he was going to kill me."

Christ, if you can't say anything, Valdez thought, quit talking.

He said, "It isn't your fault this has happened. I mean, you are made to suffer and yet you did nothing to cause it. You understand?"

The woman nodded slightly, looking into the fire now. "All right, we can't give him back to you, but we should give you something. You take something from a person, then you have to pay for it. We have to pay. We have to pay you for taking your husband. You see that?"

The woman did not move or speak.

"I don't know how much you pay a woman for killing her husband, but we'll think of something, all right? There were many men there; I don't know them all. But the ones I know I go to and ask them to give me something for you. A hundred dollars. No, *five* hundred dollars we get and give it to you so you can do what you want with it. Have your baby and go home, wherever your home is, or stay here. Buy some, I don't know, something to grow, and a cow and maybe some goats, uh? You know goats?"

Christ, let her buy what she wants. Get it done.

"Look," Valdez said then. "We get in the wagon and

go back to town. I see the men and talk to them—you stay in town also. I find a place for you, all right?"

The woman's gaze rose from the fire, her dark face glistening in the light, the shapeless, flat-faced Lipan Apache woman looking at him. A person, but Christ, barely a person.

Why did Rincón choose this one? Valdez thought. He smiled then. "How does that sound? You stay in town, sleep in a bed. You don't have to worry or think about it. We pay for everything."

A Maricopa rider came into De Spain's, where Mr. Beaudry and Mr. Malson were playing poker with another gentleman and the house man, and told them it was the goddamedest thing he'd seen in a while: Bob Valdez walking into the Republic Hotel with that blown-up Indian woman.

R. L. Davis came over from the bar and said, "What about the Indian woman? Hell, I could have knocked her flat if I'd wanted. Nobody believes that then they never seen me shoot."

Mr. Malson told him to shut up and said to the Maricopa rider, "What's this about Bob Valdez?"

"He's in the Republic registering that nigger's squaw," the rider said. "I saw them come up in the team and go inside, so I stuck my head in."

Mr. Beaudry was squinting in his cigar smoke. "What'd the clerk do?"

"I guess he didn't know what to do," the rider said. "He went and got the manager, and him and Bob Valdez were talking over the counter, but I couldn't hear them."

Mr. Malson, the manager of Maricopa, looked at Mr.

Beaudry, the government land agent, and Mr. Beaudry said, "I never heard of anything like that before."

Mr. Malson shook his head. "They won't give her a room. Christ Almighty."

Mr. Beaudry shook his head too. "I don't know," he said. "Bob Valdez. You sure it was Bob?"

"Yes sir," the Maricopa rider said. He waited a minute while the men at the poker table thought about it, then went over to the bar and got himself a glass of whiskey.

Next to him, R. L. Davis said, "Were you out there today?" The rider shook his head, but said he'd heard all about it. R. L. Davis told him how he had taken the Winchester and put four good ones right behind the woman when she came out for water and one smack in the door as she went back inside. "Hell," R. L. Davis said, "I'd wanted to hit her I'd have hit her square."

The Maricopa rider said, "God*dam*, I guess she's a big enough something to shoot at for anybody."

"I was two hundred yards off!" R. L. Davis stiffened up and his face was tight. "I put them shots right where I aimed!"

The Maricopa rider said, "All right, I believe you." He was tired and didn't feel like arguing with some stringy drunk who was liable to make something out of nothing.

For a Saturday night there was only a fair crowd in De Spain's, the riders and a few town merchants lined up and lounged at the bar and some others played poker and faro, with tobacco smoke hanging above them around the brass lamps. They were drinking and talking, but it didn't seem loud enough for a Saturday.

There had been more men in here earlier, right after
supper, a number of them coming in for a quick glass
or a jug to take with them, heading back to their
spreads with their families, but now it was only a fair-
sized crowd. The moment of excitement had been Mr.
Tanner coming in. He had stood at the bar and lit a
cigar and sipped two glasses of whiskey while Mr. Malson stood with him. Those who were out at the Maricopa pasture pointed out Mr. Tanner to those who
hadn't been there. The reactions to seeing him were
mostly the same. So that was Frank Tanner. He didn't
look so big. They expected a man with his name and
reputation to look different—a man who traded goods
to Mexican rebels and had a price on his head across
the border and two dozen guns riding for him. Imag-
ine paying all those men. He must do pretty well. He
was a little above average height and was straight as a
post, thin, with a thin, sunken-in face and a heavy
moustache and eyes in the shadow of his hatbrim. He
made a person look at him when he walked in, but
once the person had looked, Tanner wasn't that different from anybody else. That was the reaction to Frank
Tanner. That he was not so much after all. Still, while
he was in De Spain's, it seemed quieter, like everybody
was holding back, though most of the men were trying
to act natural and somebody would laugh every once
in a while. Frank Tanner stayed fifteen minutes and
left. He'd gone over to the Republic and shortly after,
he and his wife were seen riding out of Lanoria in their
buggy with a mounted Mexican trailing them, everyone coming to doors and windows to get a look at
them. The men said boy, his wife was something—a

nice young thing and not too frail either, and the women admitted yes, she was pretty, but she ought to knot or braid her hair instead of letting it hang down like that; it made her look awful bold.

Frank Tanner had left De Spain's over two hours ago. Now, the next one to come in, just a little while after the Maricopa rider, was Bob Valdez.

The house man saw him and nudged Mr. Malson under the table. Mr. Malson looked at him funny, frowning—What was the little bald-headed son of a bitch up to?—then saw the house man looking toward the door. Bob Valdez was coming directly toward their table, his gaze already picking out Mr. Malson, who looked at him and away from him and back again, and Bob Valdez was still looking right at him.

"I buried him," Valdez said.

Mr. Malson nodded. "Good. There were enough witnesses, I didn't see any need for an inquest." He looked up at Bob Valdez. "Everybody knows how he died."

"Unless his wife wants him buried at home," Valdez said.

Mr. Beaudry said, "Let her move him if she wants. Phew, driving that team in the sun with him on the back. How'd you like to do that?"

R. L. Davis, who had moved over from the bar, said, "I guess that boy stunk enough when he was alive." He looked around and got a couple of the riders to laugh at it.

"I haven't asked her if she wants to," Valdez said. "It's something she'll think about later when she's home. But I told her one thing," he said then. "I told her we'd pay her for killing her husband."

There was a silence at the table. Mr. Beaudry fooled with the end of his moustache, twisting it, and Mr. Malson cleared his throat before he said, "We? Who's we?"

"I thought everybody who was there," Bob Valdez said. "Or everybody who wants to give something."

Mr. Malson said, "You mean take up a collection? Pass the hat around?"

Valdez nodded. "Yes sir."

"Well, I suppose we could do that." He looked at Beaudry. "What do you think, Earl?"

Mr. Beaudry shrugged. "I don't care. I guess it would be all right. Give her a few dollars for a stake."

Mr. Malson nodded. "Enough to get home. Where does she live?"

"Their place is north of here," Valdez said.

"No, I mean where is she from?"

"I don't know."

"Probably across the border," Mr. Beaudry said. "She could collect about ten dollars and it'd be more than any of her kin had ever seen before."

Mr. Malson said, "I suppose we could do it."

"I was thinking of more than ten dollars," Valdez said.

Mr. Malson looked up at him. "How much more?"

Bob Valdez cleared his throat. He said, "I was thinking five hundred dollars."

The silence followed again. This time R. L. Davis broke it. He moved, shifting his weight, and there was a chinging sound of his spurs. He said, "I would like to know something. I would like to know why we're listening to this greaser. It was him killed the nigger. What's he coming to us for?"

"R. L.," Mr. Malson said, "keep your mouth closed, all right?"

"Why can't I say what I want?" R. L. Davis said, drunk enough to tell the manager of Maricopa to his face, "He killed him. Not us."

Mr. Malson said, "Shut up or go to bed." He took his time shifting his gaze to Bob Valdez, then holding it there, staring at him. "That's a lot of money, five hundred dollars."

"Yes sir," Bob Valdez nodded, speaking quietly. "I guess it is, but she needs it. What does she have now? I mean, we take her husband from her and now she doesn't have anything. So I thought five hundred dollars." He smiled a little. "It just came to me. That much."

Mr. Beaudry said, "That's as much as most men make in a year."

"Yes sir," Bob Valdez said. "But her husband won't earn anything anymore. Not this year or any year. So maybe five hundred is not so much."

Mr. Beaudry said, "Giving that much is different than giving her a few dollars. I don't mean the difference in the amount. I mean you give her a sum like five hundred dollars it's like admitting we owe it to her. Like we're to blame."

"Well?" Bob Valdez said. "Who else is to blame?"

Mr. Beaudry said, "Now wait a minute. If you're anxious to fix blame then I'll have to go along with what this man said." He nodded toward R. L. Davis.

"You killed him. We didn't. We were there to help flush him out, a suspected murderer. We weren't there to kill anybody unless we had to. But you took it on yourself to go down and talk to him and it was you that killed him. Am I right or wrong?"

Bob Valdez said, "Everybody was shooting——"

Mr. Beaudry held up his hand. "Wait just a minute. Shooting isn't killing. Nobody's shot killed him but yours and there are ninety, a hundred witnesses will testify to it."

"I said it before," R. L. Davis said. "He killed the coon. Nobody else. The wrong coon at that."

A few of them laughed and Bob Valdez looked over at R. L. Davis standing with his funneled hat over his eyes and his thumbs hooked in his belt trying to stand straight but swaying a little. He was good and drunk, his eyes watery looking and the corners of his mouth sticky. But it would be good to hit him anyway, Bob Valdez was thinking. Come in from the side and get his cheek and rip into his nose without hitting those ugly teeth and maybe cut your hand. With gloves on hit the mouth, but not without gloves. He could see R. L. Davis sitting on the floor of De Spain's saloon with his nose bleeding and blood down the front of him. That would be all right.

And who else? No, he should be able to talk to Mr. Malson and Mr. Beaudry, the manager of a cattle company and a government land agent, but he was having one son of a bitch of a hard time because they didn't see it, what he meant, or they didn't want to see it.

He said, "I mean this way. What if she went to court——"

"Jesus Christ," R. L. Davis said, shaking his head.

"What if she went there"—Valdez kept his eyes on Mr. Beaudry now—"with a lawyer and said she wanted to sue everybody that was out there, or this city?"

"Bob," Mr. Beaudry said, "that woman doesn't know what a lawyer is."

"But if she did and they went to court, wouldn't she get some money?"

The house man said, "I thought we were playing cards."

"Since she's never heard of a lawyer or a county seat," Mr. Beaudry said, "you're talking straight into the wind, aren't you?"

"I mean if she did. Like if you drive cattle over a man's property and damage something," Bob Valdez went on, holding on, "and the man goes to court, then the cattle company has to pay him for the damage. Isn't that right?"

Mr. Malson smiled. He said, "That doesn't sound like much of a cattle company to me," and the others laughed. "I was to get involved in court suits, a man would be out from Chicago and I'd be out of a job."

"But it's happened," Valdez said, staying with it. "The person or persons responsible have had to pay."

Mr. Beaudry said, "I wouldn't worry about it, Bob."

"The person has to stand up and prove damage," Mr. Malson said. "You don't go to court, even if you know where it is, without a case. And by that I mean evidence."

"All right," Valdez said. "That's what I mean. The woman doesn't know anything about court, but we know about the evidence, uh? Because we were there. If we weren't there her husband would be alive.''

"Or if he hadn't opened the door," Mr. Beaudry said. "Or if you hadn't pulled the trigger."

"Or," Mr. Malson said, "if he hadn't come to town this morning and if Frank Tanner hadn't seen him."

"Goddam, I was there," R. L. Davis said. "We was on the steps of the Republic."

"There you are," Mr. Beaudry said. "If Frank Tanner hadn't been here this morning it never would have happened. So maybe it's his fault. Tanner's."

Somebody in the group behind Mr. Beaudry said, "Go tell him that," and some of the men laughed, picturing it.

"Now that's not so funny," Mr. Beaudry said. "If this happened because of Frank Tanner, then maybe he's to blame. What do you think, Bob?" he asked him seriously, patiently, as he would ask a stupid, thick-headed person.

"I guess so," Bob Valdez said.

"Well, if you think he's to blame," Mr. Beaudry said, "why don't you ask him for the money? And I'll tell you what. If he agrees to the five hundred dollars, we will too. How's that?"

Valdez kept his eyes on Mr. Beaudry. "I don't know where he is."

"He's south of town," Mr. Beaudry said. "Probably at the relay station for the night if his cattle got that far. Or he might have gone on."

"He mentioned stopping there," Mr. Malson said.

"All right," Valdez said because there was nothing else he could say. "I'll go talk to him."

"Do that," Mr. Beaudry said.

Mr. Malson waited until Bob Valdez was turning and the men who had crowded in were stepping aside. "Bob," he said, "that Apache woman—somebody said she was over to the hotel trying to get a room."

"No." Valdez shook his head. "The manager said they were full up."

"Uh-huh," Mr. Malson said. "Well, where is she now?"

"I took her to Inez's place," Valdez said. "She's staying there tonight."

Nobody said anything until he was gone. Then R. L. Davis, as drunk as he was, said, "Je-sus H. Christ. Now he's turned that Indin creature into a whore."

He went unarmed, riding south through the darkness, feeling the chill of night settling on the land. He didn't want to go; he was tired. He had come up this road this morning from St. David on the bouncing, bucking, creaking boot of the Hatch and Hodges stage, throwing gravel at the wheelers and yelling, urging the horses on as the driver held the heavy reins and snapped them over the teams. Sun and dust this morning, and sweat soaking his body under the dark suit; now cold darkness over the same ruts that stretched across the mesquite flats and climbed through barrancas to crest a hill and drop curving into the endless flats again, forever, it seemed, on the boot or now in the saddle of a stage company horse.

He said in his mind, Mr. Tanner, I'm Bob Valdez. You remember, I was out at the pasture today when the man was killed.

When the man was killed. When *you* killed him, he said to himself.

We were talking about doing something for his wife and Mr. Beaudry, the land agent, said——

He said go out and try to get it from Frank Tanner, you dumb Mexican son of a bitch. That's what he said. Do you know it?

He knew it. Sure. But what was he supposed to do? Forget about the woman? He had told her they would give her money. God, it would be easy to forget about her. No, it would be good, but it wouldn't be easy. But with all of them watching him he had had to walk out and get a horse and he would have to ride the ten goddam miles or more to the goddam swing station and, getting it over with, smile and be respectful and ask Mr. Tanner if he would please like to give something for this fat squaw who had lived with Rincón and was having his child.

And Frank Tanner, like the rest of them, would say——

No, they said this Tanner had a lot of money. Maybe he would say, "Sure, I'll give you something for her. How much do you want?" Maybe it would be easy to talk to him. Maybe now, at night, after it was over and the man had had time to think about it, maybe he would talk a little and say yes.

A mile or a little more from the stage station he saw low shapes out among the brush patches, cattle grazing, bedded for the night, and among them, the taller shape of a rider. But they were well off from the stage road and none of the cattle he saw or the mounted man came near him. During the last mile he was certain a rider was behind him, but he didn't stop or slow down to let the horse sound catch up with him. It could be somebody on the road, anybody, or one of Tanner's men watching him; but he had nothing to say to whoever it was. His words were for Tanner, even if he didn't know how to put the words to convince the man. It would be easier to say it in Spanish. Or in Chiricahua.

Now, coming over a low rise, he could see the glow of their fires, three of them, where the swing station would be in the darkness. Gradually then, as he approached, he could make out the adobe building, the fires reflecting on pale walls in the night. The front of the building, beneath the mesquite-pole ramada, was in deep shadow. Closer now and he could see the low adobe outer wall across the front yard, shielding the well and the horse corral from open country.

Valdez listened as he approached. He could hear the men by the fire, the thin sound of voices coming across the yard. He could hear horses moving in the corral and a shrill whinnying sound. He was aware of horses closer to him, off in the darkness, but moving in with the heavy muffled sound of hooves on the packed sand. He did not look toward the sound but continued on, coming to the wall and walking his horse through the open gate, feeling the riders out of the darkness close behind him as he entered the yard.

A figure by the wall with a rifle said, "Hold it there," and a voice behind him, in English also but with an accent said, "We have him." The man with the rifle came toward him, raising the barrel of a Henry or a Winchester—Valdez wasn't sure in the dimness.

He said in Spanish, "I have no gun."

And the voice behind him said, also in Spanish, "Get down and show us."

Valdez swung down. He dropped the reins and opened his coat as the man with the rifle, a Winchester, came up to him.

"The saddle," the voice behind him said in English.

Not looking around Valdez said, "You make sure, don't you?" The man behind him didn't answer. He walked his horse forward and dismounted close to Valdez, looking into his face.

"You go where?"

"Here," Valdez said. "To speak to Señor Tanner."

"About what?"

"Money," Valdez said.

The man who had dismounted continued to study him for a moment. He handed his reins to the one with the rifle and walked off toward the adobe. Valdez watched him and saw the men by the fires, on the side of the adobe, looking out toward him. It was quiet now except for the stirring of the horses in the corral. He saw the light in the doorway as the man went inside. The door remained open, but he could see nothing within.

There was a bar inside the room and two long tables. The station man, Gregario Sanza, would be behind the bar maybe, serving Tanner. He remembered Tanner did not take anything to drink at the pasture.

He said to the one with the rifle, "The company I work for owns that building. The Hatch and Hodges."

The man said nothing. Beyond him now two figures appeared in the doorway, in the light for a moment and out of it into darkness. Not Tanner, neither of them. The one who had gone inside called out, "Bring him over." The two men in shadow came out a few steps and the second one, also with an accent, said, "Against the wall," motioning with a nod of his head to the side.

Some of the men by the fires had stood up or were rising as Valdez walked toward them. Others sat and lounged on their sides—dark faces, dark leather, firelight reflecting on cartridge belts and mess tins—and Valdez had to walk around them to reach the wall. As he turned, the man who had come out of the house walked over to stand across the fire from him, the men standing or sitting there quickly making room for him.

The *segundo*, Valdez thought. They move.

He was a big man, almost as big as Diego Luz, with a straw Sonora hat and a heavy moustache that gave him a solemn expression and a strip of beard beneath his mouth. The segundo, with one cartridge bandolier and two long-barreled .44s on his legs.

Valdez nodded to him and said in Spanish, "Good evening," almost smiling.

"I don't know you," the segundo said.

"Because we have never met."

"I know everyone who does business with Señor Tanner."

"I have no business with him. A private matter."

"You told them business."

"I told them money."

The segundo was silent, watching him. "He doesn't know you," he said then.

"Señor Tanner? Sure, I met him today. I killed a man for him."

The segundo hesitated again, undecided or taking his own time, watching him. He motioned with his hand then, and the Mexican who had gone into the house before moved away, turning the corner. The segundo continued to stare. Valdez shifted his gaze to the left and to the right and saw all of them watching him in the light of the fires. There were Americans and Mexicans, some of them bearded, most of them with their hats on, all of them armed. He counted, looking about idly, and decided there were at least twelve of them here. More of them out in the darkness.

He said in his mind, Mr. Tanner, do you remember me? Bob——

Tanner came around the corner. He took a stub of cigar out of his mouth and stood looking at Valdez.

Now. "Mr. Tanner, do you remember me? Bob Valdez, from the pasture today."

Tanner held the cigar in front of him. He was in his shirtsleeves and vest and without the dark hat that had hidden his eyes, his hair slanting down across his forehead, the skin pale-looking in the firelight. He seemed thinner now and smaller, but his expression was the same, the tell-nothing expression and the mouth that looked as if it had never smiled.

"What do you want?"

"I just wanted to talk to you for a minute."

"Say it."

"Well, it's about the man today."

"What man?"

"The one that was killed. You know he had a wife with him." Valdez waited.

"Say what you want and get out of here."

"Well, we were talking—Mr. Beaudry and Mr. Malson. You know who I mean?"

"You don't have much time left," Mr. Tanner said.

"We were saying maybe we should give something to the woman now that she doesn't have a husband."

"They sent you out here?"

"No, I thought of it. I thought if we all put in to give her some money"—he hesitated—"about five hundred dollars."

Mr. Tanner had not moved his gaze from Valdez. "You come out here to tell me that?"

"Well, we were talking about it and Mr. Beaudry said why don't I see you about it."

"You want me to pay money," Mr. Tanner said, "to that red nigger he was holed up with?"

"You said it wasn't the right man——"

"What's that got to do with it?"

"It was an accident, not the woman's fault, and she doesn't have anything now. And she's got that child she's going to have. Did you see that?"

Mr. Tanner looked at his segundo. He said, "Get rid of him," and started to turn away.

"Wait a minute!"

Valdez watched him half turn to look at him again.

"What did you say?"

"I mean if you could take time to listen a minute so I can explain it." The hard-working, respectful Bob Valdez speaking again, smiling a little.

"Your minute's up, boy." He glanced at his segundo

again. "Teach him something." He turned and was gone.

Valdez called out, "Mr. Tanner——"

"He don't hear you so good," the segundo said. "It's too loud out here." He drew the .44 on his right leg, cocked it and fired as he brought it up, and with the explosion the adobe chipped next to Bob Valdez's face.

"All this shooting," the segundo said. "Man, he can't hear anything." He fired again and the adobe chipped close to the other side of Valdez's face. "You see how easy it would be?" the segundo said.

The Mexican rider who had brought him in said, "Let me have one," his revolver already drawn. "Where do you want it?"

"By the right hand," the segundo said.

Valdez was looking at the Mexican rider. He saw the revolver lift as the man pulled the trigger and saw the muzzle flash with the heavy solid noise and heard the bullet strike close to his side.

"Too high," the segundo said.

Now those who were sitting and lounging by the fires rose and drew their revolvers, looking at the segundo and waiting their turn. One of them, an American, said, "I know where I'm going to shoot the son of a bitch." One of them laughed and another one said, "See if you can shoot his meat off." And another one said, "It would fix this squaw-lover good."

Bob Valdez did not want to move. He wanted to run and he could feel the sweat on his face, but he couldn't move a hand or an elbow or turn his head. He had to stay rigid without appearing to be rigid. He edged his left foot back and the heel of his boot touched the wall close behind him. He did that much, touching something solid and holding on, as the men faced him across the fires, five or six strides away from him, close enough to put the bullets where they wanted to put them—if all of the men knew how to shoot and if they hadn't had too much mescal or tequila since coming to the station. Valdez held on and now kept his eyes on the segundo for a place to keep them, a point to fix on while they played their game with him.

The first few men fired in turn, calling their shots; but now the rest of them were anxious and couldn't wait and they began firing as they decided where to shoot, raising the revolvers in front of them but not seeming to aim, pulling the triggers in the noise and smoke and leaning in to see where their bullets struck. Valdez felt his hat move and felt powder dust from the adobe brick in his eyes and in his nose and felt chips of adobe sting his face and hands and felt a bullet plow into the wall between his knees and a voice say, "A little higher you get him good." Another voice, "Move up a inch at a time and watch him poop his drawers."

He kept his eyes on the segundo in the Sonora straw, not telling the segundo anything with his gaze, looking at him as he would look at any man, if he wanted to look at the man, or as he would look at a horse or a dog or a steer or an object that was something to look at. But as he saw the segundo staring back at him he realized that he was telling the segundo something after all. Good. He had nothing to lose and now was aware of himself staring at the segundo.

What can you do? he was saying to the segundo. You can kill me. Or one of them can kill me not meaning to.

But what else can you do to me? You want me to get down on my knees? You don't have enough bullets, man, and you know it. So what can you do to me? Tell me.

The segundo raised his hand and called out, "Enough!" in English and in Spanish and in English again. He walked between the fires to Bob Valdez and said, "You ride out now."

Bob Valdez took his hat off, adjusting it, loosening it on his head. He didn't touch his face to wipe away the brick dust and sweat or look at his hands, though he felt blood on his knuckles and running down between his fingers.

He said, "If you're through," and walked away from the segundo. He mounted the company horse and rode out the gate, the segundo watching him until he was into the darkness and only a faint sound of him remained.

The men were talking and reloading, spinning the cylinders of their revolvers, sitting by the fires to rest and to tell where they had put their bullets. The segundo walked away from them out into the yard, listening to the silence. After a few minutes he went under the ramada to enter the adobe.

The station man, Gregorio Sanza, behind the plank bar and beneath the smoking oil lamp, raised a mescal bottle to the segundo, pale yellow in the light; but the segundo shook his head; he walked over to the long table where Tanner was sitting with the woman. She was sipping a tin cup of coffee.

The woman had gone into a sleeping room shortly

after they had arrived in the buggy and had remained there until now. The segundo saw she was still dressed and he wondered what she had been doing in the room. In the months she had been with them—since Tanner had brought her over from Fort Huachuca— the segundo could count the times he had spoken to her on his hands. She seldom asked for anything; she never gave the servants orders as the woman of the house was supposed to do. Still, she had the look of a woman who would be obeyed. She did not seem afraid or uneasy; she looked into your eyes when she spoke to you; she spoke loud enough yet quietly. But something was going on in her head beneath the long gold-brown hair that hung past her shoulders. She was a difficult woman to understand because she did not give herself away. Except that she smiled only a little, and he had never seen her laugh. Maybe she laughed when she was alone with Señor Tanner.

If she was my woman, the segundo was thinking, I could make her laugh and scream and bite.

He said to Tanner, "The man's gone."

"How did he behave?"

"He stood up."

Tanner drew on the fresh cigar he was smoking. "He did, uh?"

"As well as a man can do it."

"He didn't beg?"

The segundo shook his head. "He said nothing."

"He shot the nigger square," Tanner said. "He did that well. But outside, I thought he would crawl."

The segundo shook his head again. "No crawling or begging."

"All right, tell that man to close his bar and go to bed."

The segundo nodded and moved off.

Tanner waited until the segundo had stopped at the bar and had gone outside. "Why don't you go to bed, too," he said to the woman.

"I will in a minute." She kept her finger in the handle of the coffee cup.

"Go in and pretty yourself up," he said then. "I'll take a turn around the yard and be in directly."

"What did the man do?"

"He wasted my time."

"So they put him against the wall?"

"It was the way he spoke to me," Tanner said. "I can't have that in front of them." He sat close to her, staring into her face, at the gray-green eyes and the soft hair close to her cheek. His hand came up to finger the end strands of her hair. Quietly, he said, "Gay, go on in the room."

"I'll finish my coffee."

"No, right now would be better. I'll be there in a minute."

She waited until he was out of the door before rising and going into the sleeping room. In the dim lamplight she began to undress, stepping out of her dress and dropping it on the bed next to her nightgown. The light blue one. Thin and limp and patched beneath one arm. There had been a light blue one and a light green one and a pink one and a yellow one, all with the white-scrolled monogram GBE she had embroidered on the bodice when she was nineteen years old and living in Prescott, a girl about to be married. The girl, Gay

Byrnes, had brought the nightgowns and her dresses and linens to Fort Huachuca to become the bride of James C. Erin. During five and a half years as his wife she discarded the nightgowns one by one and used them as dust rags. When her husband was killed six months ago, and she left Huachuca with Frank Tanner, she had only the light blue one left.

Gay Erin slipped the nightgown over her head, brushed her hair and got into the narrow double bed, pulling the blanket up over her shoulder as she rolled to her side, her back to the low-burning lamp.

When Tanner came in and began to undress, she remained with her back to him. She could see him from times before: removing his boots, his shirt and trousers, standing in his long cotton underwear as he unfastened the buttons. He would stand naked scratching his stomach and chest, then go to the wall hook and take his revolver from the holster, making sure the hammer was on an empty chamber as he moved toward the bed.

She felt the mattress yield beneath his weight. The gun would be at his side, under the blanket and next to his hip. He would lie still for a few moments, then roll toward her and put his hand on her shoulder.

"What have you got the nightgown on for?"

"I'm cold."

"Well now, what do you think I'm for?"

"Tell me," Gay Erin said.

"I'll show you."

"As a lover or a husband?"

Tanner groaned. "Jesus Christ, are you going to start that?"

"Six months ago you said we'd be married in a few weeks."

"Most people probably think we already are. What's the difference?"

She started to get up, to throw back the blanket, and his hand tightened on her arm.

"I said we'd be married, we will."

"When?"

"Well not right now, all right?" His hand stroked her arm beneath the flannel. "Come on, take this thing off."

She lay without moving, her eyes open in the darkness, letting her hesitation stretch into silence, a long moment, before she sat up slowly and worked the nightgown out from beneath her. She pulled it over her head, turning to him.

THREE

●

Inez was fat and took her time coming over from the stove with the coffeepot. Filling the china cup in front of Bob Valdez and then her own, Inez said, "She left early. It must have been before daybreak."

"You hear her?"

"No, maybe one of the girls did. I can ask."

"It doesn't matter."

"I heard what you're doing," Inez said.

"Well, I'm not doing very good. I wanted to tell the woman maybe it would take me a little longer."

"You're crazy."

"Listen, I'm tired," Valdez said. "I'm not going to argue with you, all right?"

"Go upstairs."

"I said I'm tired."

"So are the girls. I mean take a room and go to sleep."

"I have a run to St. David this afternoon and don't come back till the morning."

"Tell them you're sick."

"No, they don't have anybody."

"That Davis was in here last night. I threw him out."

"You can do it," Valdez said.

"He was in no condition. Only talk. I don't need talk," Inez said. She made a noise sipping her coffee and watched Valdez shape a cigarette. He handed it to her and made another one and lit them with a kitchen match.

"Now what do you do, forget the whole thing?"

"I don't know." He rubbed a gnarled brown hand over his hair, pulling it down on his forehead. "I think maybe talk to this Mr. Tanner again."

"You're crazy."

"I didn't explain it to him right. The part that it's like a court where you get money for something done to you. Not like a court, but, you know."

"You're still crazy. He won't listen to you. Nobody will."

"But if he does, the others will, uh?" Valdez sipped his coffee.

"Put a gun in his back if you can get close to him," Inez said. "That's the only way."

"No guns."

"The little shotgun."

Valdez nodded, thinking about it. "That would be good, wouldn't it?"

"Boom!" Inez laughed out and the sound of her voice filled the kitchen.

Valdez smiled. "Has he ever been in here?"

"They say he's got a woman. Maybe he beats her or does strange things to her."

"He's never been here, but you don't like him," Valdez said. "Why?"

"My book."

"Ah, your book. I forgot about it."

"You're in it."

"Sure, I remember now."

Inez called out, "Polly!" and waited a moment and called again.

A dark-haired girl in a robe came through the door from the front room. She smiled at Bob Valdez, holding the robe together in front of her. "Early bird," she said.

"No early bird. Get me the book," Inez said.

"Which, the black one?"

"No, the one before," Inez said. "The green one."

Valdez shook his head. "Black ones and green ones. How many do you have?"

"They go back about twelve years. To your time."

"Like I'm an old man now."

"Sometime you act it."

The girl came into the kitchen again with the scrap-book under her arm. "The green one," she said, winking at Bob Valdez and handing it to Inez, who pushed her coffee cup out of the way to open the book on the table. Inez sat at the end of the kitchen table with Polly standing behind her now, looking over her shoulder. Sitting to the side, Valdez lowered and cocked his head to look at the newspaper clippings and photographs mounted in the book.

"He seems familiar," Valdez said.

Inez looked at him. "I hope so. It's Rutherford Hayes."

"Well, that was twelve, fourteen years ago," Valdez said. He looked up as Polly laughed. She was leaning over Inez and the top of her robe hung partly open.

There were photographs of local businessmen, territorial officials and national figures, including two presidents, Rutherford Hayes and Chester A. Arthur, Profirio Díaz and Carmelita at Niagara Falls, and the Prince of Wales on his visit to Washington.

"Have they been to your place?" Valdez asked.

"No, but if they come I want to recognize them." Inez turned a page. "Earl Beaudry, on his appointment as land agent." Inez moved to the next page, her finger tracing down the column of newspaper clippings.

"Here it is," she said. "The first mention of him. August 13, 1881—Frank Tanner and a Carlisle Baylor were convicted of cattle theft and sent to Yuma Penitentiary."

Valdez seemed as pleased as he was surprised. "He's been to prison."

"For a few years, I think," Inez said. "It doesn't say how long. He was stealing cattle and driving them across the border. There's more about him." Her hand moved down the column and went to the next page. "Here, October, 1886, Frank J. Tanner, cattle broker, arraigned on a charge of murder in Contention, Arizona."

"Cattle broker now," Valdez said.

"The case was dismissed."

"It's getting better."

Inez turned the page. "Ah, here's the picture. You see him there?" Inez turned the book halfway toward

Valdez and he leaned in, recognizing Tanner standing with a group of Army officers in front of an adobe building.

Inez read the caption. "It says he has a contract with the government to supply remounts to the Tenth United States Cavalry at Fort Huachuca." She turned a few more pages. "I think that's all."

"Nothing about him now, uh?"

"There's something else sticks in my mind about Huachuca," Inez said, "but I don't see it. Unless— sure, it would be in the other book." She sat back in her chair looking up over her shoulder. "Polly?"

Valdez watched the girl straighten and draw the robe together.

"Should I take this one?" the girl asked.

Inez was turning pages again. "No, I want to show Bob something."

"What have you got now?" he asked her.

Coming to a page, she pressed it flat and turned the book to him. "You remember?"

Valdez smiled a little. "That one."

It was a photograph of Bob Valdez taken at Fort Apache, Arizona, September 7, 1884: Bob Valdez standing among small trees and cactus plants the photographer had placed in his studio shed as a background: Bob Valdez with a Sharps .50 cradled in one arm and a long-barreled Walker Colt on his leg. He was wearing a hat, with a bandana beneath it that covered half of his forehead, a belt of cartridges for the Sharps, and knee-length Apache moccasins. The caption beneath the picture described Roberto Valdez as chief of scouts with Major General George Crook, Department of Arizona, during his expedition into Sonora against hostile Apaches.

"That's the way I still picture you," Inez said. "When someone says Bob Valdez, this is the one I see. Not the one that wears a suit and a collar."

Valdez was concentrating on the book, looking now at a photograph of a young Apache scout in buckskins and holding a rifle, standing against the same background used in the photo of himself. He remembered the photographer, a man named Fly. And the day the pictures were taken at Fort Apache. He remembered the scout washing himself and brushing his hair and putting on the buckskin shirt he had bought and had never worn before.

"Peaches," Valdez said. "General Crook's guide. His real name was Tso-ay, but the soldiers and the general called him Peaches. His skin." Valdez continued to study the photograph. He said, "They'd put a suit and a collar on him too, if they ever took his picture again."

Inez looked up as Polly came in with the other scrapbook. She took it from her and held it over the table.

"I don't know where he is now," Valdez was saying. "Maybe Fort Sill, Oklahoma, with the rest of them. Planting corn." He shook his head. "Man, I would like to see that sometime. Those people growing things in a garden."

Inez opened the book and laid it over the page Valdez was studying. He sat back as she turned a few pages and raised his gaze to Polly, who was looking over Inez's shoulder again, letting her robe come open. She was built very well and had very white skin.

"Here it is," Inez said. "Sutler murdered at Fort Huachuca. James C. Erin was found shot to death a few miles from the fort today——"

Valdez stopped her. "When was this?"

Inez looked at the date on the clipping. "March. Six months ago."

"That's the one Orlando Rincón was supposed to have killed."

"It says he was found by some soldiers and"—her finger moved down the column—"here's the part. 'Held for questioning was Frank J. Tanner of Mimbreño, said to be the last person to have seen Erin alive. Mr. Tanner stated he had spent the previous evening with Mr. and Mrs. Erin at the fort, but had left for a business appointment in Nogales and had not seen Erin on the day he was reported to have been killed.' "

"He was sure it was Rincón," Valdez said. "And that his name was Johnson."

Inez nodded, looking at the book. "They mention a Johnson, listed as a deserter and also a suspect. A trooper with the Tenth Cavalry."

"Maybe they know this Johnson did it now," Valdez said.

Inez looked over the pages facing her. "I don't see anything more about it."

Valdez raised his eyes from the open robe to the nice-looking face of the dark-haired girl. "It's too bad he doesn't come here," he said.

Inez closed the book. "He never has and I would guess he knows where it is."

"If he did," Valdez said, his gaze still on Polly. "I could wait for him."

* * *

Diego Luz had a dream in which he saw himself sitting on a corral fence watching his men working green horses in the enclosure. In the dream, which he would look at during the day as well as at night, Diego Luz was manager of the Maricopa Cattle Company. He lived with his family in the whitewashed adobe off beyond the corral, where the cedars stood against the sky: a house with trees and a stone well in the yard and a porch to sit on in the evening. Sometimes he would picture himself on the porch with his family about him, his three sons and two daughters, his wife and his wife's mother and whatever relatives might be visiting them. But his favorite dream was to see himself on the corral fence with his eldest son, who was almost a man, sitting next to him.

The hands were very nervous when he watched them with the horses because they knew he was the greatest mustanger and horsebreaker who ever lived. They knew he could subdue the meanest animals and they were afraid to make mistakes in his presence. He had told them how to do it, what they must do and not do, and he liked to watch them at work.

In the dream Diego and his son would watch R. L. Davis hanging on to the crow-hopping bronc until finally they saw him thrown and land hard on his shoulder. His son would shake his head and say, "Should I do it, Papa?" But he would say no, it was good for the man. He made R. L. Davis ride only the rough string, the outlaws and spoiled horses, when they were on roundup or a drive, and made R. L. Davis call him Señor Luz.

R. L. Davis mounted the bronc and was thrown
again and this time he went after the horse with a
loaded quirt and began beating the animal over the
head. At this point in the dream Diego Luz walked over
to R. L. Davis and said to him, "Hey," and when R. L.
Davis looked around Diego Luz hit him in the face
with one of his big fists. R. L. Davis went down and the
eldest son poured a bucket of water on him and when
the man shook his head and opened his eyes, he said,
"What did I do?" Diego Luz said, "You hit the horse."
R. L. Davis frowned, holding his jaw. "But you hit
them when you broke horses," he said. And Diego Luz
smiled and said, "Maybe, but now I hit whoever I want
to."

R. L. Davis was a good one to hit. Once in a while
though, he would leave R. L. Davis alone and hit Mr.
Malson, not hitting him too hard, but letting him know
he was hit. And sometimes he would fire Mr. Malson,
call him over and say, "It's too bad, but you're too
goddam weak and stupid to do this work anymore so
we got to get rid of you. And don't come back."

Diego Luz would think of these things as he worked
his land and broke the mustangs he and his eldest son
drove down out of the high country. His place was
southeast of Lanoria, well off the road to St. David and
only a few miles from the village of Mimbreño, though
there was no wagon road in that direction, only a few
trails if a man knew where to find them.

His place was adobe with straw blinds that rolled
down to cover the doorway and windows and an open
lean-to built against the house for cooking. There were
a few chickens and two goats in the yard with the three

youngest children and a brown mongrel dog that slept in the shade of the house most of the day. There was a vegetable garden for growing beans and peppers, and the peppers that were drying hung from the roof of the ramada that shaded the front of the house, which faced north, on high ground. Down the slope from the house was the well, and beyond it, on flat, cleared ground, the mesquite-pole corral where Diego Luz broke and trained the mustangs he flushed out of the hills. He worked here most of the time. Several times a year he drove a horse string down to the Maricopa spread near Lanoria, and he would go down there at roundup time and when they drove the cattle to Willcox.

When Bob Valdez appeared, circling the corral—two days following the incident at the pasture—Diego Luz and his eldest son were at the well, pulling up buckets of water and filling the wooden trough that ran to the corral. They stood watching Bob Valdez walking his horse toward them and waited, after greeting him, as he stepped down from the saddle and took the dipper of water Diego's son offered him.

There was no hurry. If a man rode all the way here he must have something to say, and it was good to wonder about it first and not ask him questions. Though Diego Luz had already decided Bob Valdez had not come to see them but was passing through on his way to Mimbreño. And who lived in Mimbreño? Frank Tanner. There it was. Simple.

They left the boy and climbed the slope to the house, Bob Valdez seeing the children in the yard, Diego's wife and her mother watching them from the lean-to where they were both holding corn dough, shaping tortillas. The small children ran up to them and the eldest daughter appeared now in the doorway of the house. Hey, a good looking girl now, almost a woman. Anita. She would be maybe sixteen years old. Valdez had not been up here in almost a year.

When they were in the shade and had lighted cigarettes, Diego Luz said, "There's something different about you. What is it?"

Valdez shrugged. "I'm the same. What are you talking about?"

"Your face is the same." Diego Luz squinted, studying him. Slowly then his face relaxed. "I know what it is. You don't have your collar on."

Valdez's hand went to his neck where he had tied a bandana.

"Or your suit. What is this, you're not dressed up?"

"It's too hot," Valdez said.

"It's always hot," Diego Luz said. His gaze dropped to Valdez's waist. "No gun though."

Valdez frowned. "What's the matter with you? I don't have a coat on, that's all."

"And you're going to see Mr. Tanner."

"Just to say a few things to him."

"My son rode to Lanoria yesterday. He heard about the few things you said the other night."

Valdez shook his head. "People don't have anything to talk about."

"Listen, the woman doesn't need any money. She doesn't know what it is."

"But we know," Valdez said. "I just want to ask you something about Tanner."

Diego Luz drew on his cigarette and squinted out into the sunlight, down the slope to the horse corral. "I know what others know. That's all."

"He lives in Mimbreño?"

"For about two years maybe."

"How do the people like him?"

"There are no people. Most of them left at the time of the Apache. The rest of them left when Frank Tanner come. He's there with his men," Diego Luz said, "and some of their women."

"How many men?"

"At least thirty. Sometimes more."

"Do they ever come here?"

"Sometimes they pass by."

"What do they do, anything?"

"They have a drink of water and go on."

"They never make any trouble?"

"No, they don't bother me. Never."

"Maybe because you work for Maricopa."

Diego Luz shrugged. "What do I have they would want?"

"Horses," Valdez said.

"Once they asked to buy a string. I told them to see Mr. Malson."

"Did Tanner himself come?"

"No, his segundo and some others."

"Do you know any of them?"

"No, I don't think any of them are from around here."

"Do you think that's strange?"

"No, these are guns he hires, not hands. I think they

hear of Tanner and what he pays and they come from all over to get a job with him."

"He pays good, uh?"

"You see them sometimes in St. David," Diego Luz said. "They spend the money. But you see different ones each time, so maybe he lose some in Mexico or they get a stomach full of it and quit."

"What, driving cattle?"

"Cattle and guns. He gets the guns somewhere and sneaks them over the border to people who are against Díaz and want to start a revolution. So over there the *rurales* and federal soldiers look for him and try to stop him. Everybody knows that."

"I've been learning the stageline business," Valdez said.

"Keep doing it," Diego Luz said, "and live to be an old man."

"Sometimes I feel old now." He watched the chickens pecking the hard ground and heard Diego Luz's children calling out something and laughing as they played somewhere on the other side of the house. What do you need besides this? he was thinking. To have a place, a family. Very quiet except for the children sometimes, and no trouble. No Apaches. No bandits raiding from across the border. Trees and water and a good house. The house could be fixed up better. A little work, that's all. He said, "I'll trade you. I become the horsebreaker, you work for the stage company."

Diego Luz was looking out at the yard. "You want this?"

"Why not? It's a good place."

"If I had something to do I wouldn't be here."

"You do all right," Valdez said.

"Do it forever," Diego Luz said. "See how you like it."

"Maybe sometime. After I see this Tanner."

Diego Luz was studying Valdez's horse. "You don't have a rifle either."

"What do I need it for?"

"Maybe you meet a couple of them on a trail, they don't like your face."

"I'll talk to them," Valdez said.

"Maybe they don't let you talk."

"Come on, they know who I am. I'm going there to talk, that's all."

"You talk better with a rifle," Diego Luz said. "I give you mine."

From habit, approaching the top of the rise—before he would be outlined for a moment against the sky— Bob Valdez looked back the way he had come, his eyes, half-closed in the sun's glare, holding on the rock shapes and darker patches of brush at the bottom of the draw. He sat motionless until he was sure of the movement, then dismounted and led his claybank mare off the trail to one side, up into young piñon pines.

For a few moments he did not think of the rider coming up behind him; he thought of his own reaction, the caution that had stopped him from topping the rise. There were no more Chiricahuas or White Mountain bands around here. There was nothing to worry about to keep him alert and listening and looking back as well as to the sides and ahead. But he had stopped.

Sure, habit, he thought. Something hanging on of no use to him now.

What difference did it make who the man was? The man wasn't following him. The man was riding south-east from the St. David road and must have left the road not far back to cut cross-country toward Mim-breño maybe, or to a village across the border. Sure, it could be one of Tanner's men. You can ride in with him, Valdez thought, and smiled at the idea of it. He would see who it was and maybe he would come out of the pines, giving the man some warning first, or maybe he wouldn't.

Now, as the man drew nearer, for some reason he was sure it was one of the Maricopa riders: the slouched, round-shouldered way the man sat his sad-dle, the funneled brim of his hat bobbing up and down with the walking movement of the horse.

Maybe he had known all the time who it was going to be. That was a funny thing. Because when he saw it was R. L. Davis, looking at the ground or deep in thought, the stringy, mouthy one who thought he was good with the Winchester, Valdez was not surprised, though he said to himself, Goddam. How do you like that?

He let him go by, up over the rise and out of sight, while he stayed in the pines to shape a cigarette and light it, wondering where the man was going, curious because it was this one and not someone else, and glad now of the habit that had made him look around when he did. He was sure the man had not been following him. The man would have been anxious and looking around and would have stopped before he topped the rise. But the question remained, Where was he going?

When Valdez moved out, keeping to the trees over the crest of the rise, he hung back and let the distance between them stretch to a hundred yards. He followed R. L. Davis this way for several miles until the trail came to open grazing land, and as R. L. Davis crossed toward the scrub trees and hills beyond the flats, a column of dust came down the slope toward him.

You look around, Bob Valdez thought. That habit stays with you. But you don't bring the field glasses.

He remained in the cover of the trees and, in the distance, watched three riders meet R. L. Davis and stand close to him for some time, forming a single shape until the group came apart and the riders, strung out now, one in front of Davis and two behind, rode with him into the deep shadow at the base of the far hills. He saw them briefly again up on the slope and at the crest of the hill.

They wonder about him too, Valdez thought. What do you want? Who do you want to see? They ask questions and take their jobs very seriously because they feel they're important. They should relax more, Valdez thought. He mounted the claybank again and rode out into the sunlight, holding the horse to a walk, keeping his eyes on the slope the riders came down and wondering if they had left someone there to watch.

No, they did it another way. One of them who had been with R. L. Davis came back. When Valdez was little more than halfway up the trail, following the switchbacks that climbed through the brush, he saw the mounted rider waiting for him, his horse standing across the trail.

As Valdez came on, narrowing the distance between them, he recognized the rider, the Mexican who had brought him into the yard of the stage station.

"Far enough," the Mexican said. He held a Winchester across his lap, but did not raise it. He studied Valdez, who reined in a few feet from him. "You come back again."

"I didn't finish talking to him," Valdez said.

"I think he finish with you, though."

"Let's go ask him."

"Maybe he don't want to see you," the Mexican said.

"It's about money again."

"You said that before. For the woman. He don't care anything about the woman."

"Maybe this time when I tell him."

"What do you have on you?"

"Nothing." Valdez raised his hands and dropped one of them to the stock of Diego Luz's rifle in its leather boot. "Only this."

"That could be enough," the Mexican said.

"You want it?" Valdez smiled. "You don't trust me?"

"Sure, I trust you." The Mexican raised the Winchester and motioned Valdez up the grade. "But I ride behind you."

Valdez edged past him up the trail and kept moving until he reached the top of the slope. Now he could see the village of Mimbreño across the valley, a mile from them beyond open land where Tanner's cattle grazed. Valdez had been to this village once before, the day after White Mountain Apaches had raided and killed three men and carried off a woman and burned the mission church. He remembered the blackened walls; the roof had collapsed into the church and the beams were still smoking. He remembered the people in the square when they rode in, the people watching the Apache scouts and company of cavalry and saying to themselves, Why weren't you here yesterday, you soldiers? What good are you?

As they crossed the grazing land Valdez recognized the church, the roofless shell that had never been repaired. It stood at the end of the single street of adobes where the street widened into a square and there was a well with a pump and a stone trough for watering the horses. Beyond the cluster of buildings was a stand of cottonwood trees and a stream that came down out of the high country to the east. Valdez saw the women in the trees, some of them walking this way carrying baskets of clothes. Then he was entering the street, the Mexican next to him now, with the dogs barking and the smell of wood fires, seeing the freight wagons along the adobe fronts and more horses than would ever be in a village this size. It was a village preparing to make war. It was a military camp, the base of a revolutionary army. Or the base of a heavily armed scouting force that would stay here until they were driven out. But at the same time it was not a village. Yes, there were people. There were women among the armed men, women in front of the adobes and a group of them at the well with gourds and wooden pails. But there were no children; no sound of children nor a sign of children anywhere.

"He's there waiting for you," the Mexican said.

Valdez was looking at the church. A gate of mesquite poles had been built across the arched opening of the doorway, and there were horses penned inside the enclosure. He felt the Mexican close to him, moving him to the east side of the square, to the two-story adobe with the loading platform across the front, the building that had been the village's general store and mill and grain warehouse.

Frank Tanner stood at the edge of the loading platform looking down at a group of riders, standing over them with his hands on his hips. A woman was behind him near the open doorway, not a Mexican woman, a blond-haired woman, golden hair in the sunlight hanging below her shoulders to the front of her white dress. Valdez looked at the woman until they were close to the platform and the riders sidestepped their horses to let the Mexican in, Valdez holding back now; and as they moved in among the riders he saw that one of them was the segundo. He saw R. L. Davis, then, mounted on a sorrel next to the segundo. He didn't look at Davis, who was watching him, but up at Tanner now, the man so close above him that he had to bend his head back, feeling awkward and unprotected and foolish with the woman watching him, to look at Tanner.

Tanner stared down at Valdez as if this would be enough, no words necessary. Valdez did not want to smile because he knew he would feel foolish, but he eased his expression to show he was sincere and had come here as an honest man with nothing to hide.

He said, "I'd like to talk to you once more."

"You've talked," Tanner said. "You get one time and you've had yours."

Maybe he was joking, so Valdez smiled a little bit now, though he didn't want to smile with the woman watching him. "I know you're a busy man," he said, "but you must be a fair man also, uh? I mean you have all these people working for you. You recognize the worth of things and pay a just wage. A man like that would also see when someone is owed something."

Goddam, it didn't sound right, hearing himself speaking with his goddam neck bent back and Tanner looking down at him like God in black boots and a black hat over his eyes.

"I mean if the woman was to go to the courthouse and say some men have killed my husband, by mistake, as an accident. So I think somebody should pay me for that—don't you think the court would say sure and order that we pay her something?"

"Jesus Christ," R. L. Davis said. Valdez did not look at him, but he knew it was Davis. He saw Tanner's eyes shift to the side, slide over and back to him again.

"I'm talking about what's fair," Valdez said. "I'm not trying to cheat anybody—if you think I want to take the money and run off. No, you can give it to the woman yourself. I mean have one of your men do it. I don't care who gives it to her."

Tanner continued to stare at him until finally he said, "You don't learn. I guess I have to keep teaching you."

"Tell me why you don't think she should have something," Valdez said. "You explain it to me, I understand it."

"No, I think there's only one thing you'll understand." Tanner's gaze went to his segundo. "You remember that one tried to run off with the horses?"

Valdez lowered his head to look at the segundo, who was nodding, picturing something. "The one who liked to walk," the segundo said.

Valdez heard Tanner say, "That one," and the segundo continued to nod his head, then raised it and gazed about the square.

"We can use the poles from the gate," the segundo said, looking toward the church, "and have some more cut."

Tanner was saying, "All right," and the segundo was looking at Valdez now. He nodded once.

Valdez felt the hand at his shoulder, fingers clawing into his neck as the hand clutched his bandana, and his own hands went to the horn of his saddle. He felt the Mexican's horse tight against his left leg, then moving away and the Mexican pulling him, choking him, until his hands slipped from the saddle horn and he was dragged from his horse, stumbling but not able to fall, held up by the Mexican's fist twisted in the tight fold of his neckerchief. They were around him and someone hit him in the face with a fist. It didn't hurt him, but it startled him; he was struck again on the back of the neck, then in the stomach, seeing the man close to him swing his fist and not being able to turn away from it. He went down and was kicked in the back, pushed over and pressed flat to the hard-packed ground. His hat was off now. A foot came down on his neck, pinning him, face turned to the side against the ground. Now they pulled his arms straight out to the sides and he felt a sharp pain through his shoulder blades as he was held in this position. Several minutes passed and he rested, breathing slowly to relax and not be tensed if they hit him again. Boots were close to his face. The boots moved and dust rose into his nostrils, but no one kicked him.

They placed a mesquite pole across his shoulders that extended almost a foot on either side beyond his outstretched hands and tied it with leather thongs to his wrists and neck. They placed another pole down the length of his back, from above his head to his heels, and lashed this one to the crosspole and also around his neck and body. When this was done the segundo told him all right, stand up.

Valdez could not press his hands to the ground. He raised his head, turning it, and pushed his forehead against the hardpack, arching against the pole down his spine, straining the muscles of his neck, and gradually, kicking and scraping the ground, worked his knees up under him.

"The other one didn't get up so quick," the segundo said.

Valdez was on his knees raising his body, and he was kicked hard from behind and slammed onto his face again.

"This one don't get up either," the Mexican said.

Valdez heard Tanner's voice say, "Get him out of here," and this time they let him work his way to his knees and stand up. But as he straightened, the bottom of the vertical pole struck the ground and held him in a hunched position, a man with a weight on his back, his eyes on the ground, unable to raise his head. Someone put his hat on his head, too low and tight on his fore-head.

"That way," the segundo said, nodding across the square. "The way you came."

"My horse," Valdez said.

"Don't worry about the horse," the segundo said. "We take care of."

There was nothing more to say. Valdez turned and started off, hunched over, raising his eyes and able to see perhaps twenty feet in front of him, but not able to hold his gaze in this strained position.

The segundo called after him. "Hey, don't fall on your back. You'll be like a turtle." He laughed, and some of the others laughed with him.

Frank Tanner watched the stooped figure circle the water pump and move down the street past the women who had come out of the adobes to look at him.

"You fixed him," R. L. Davis said.

Tanner's eyes shifted to Davis, sliding on him and away from him, as he had looked at him before. "I don't remember asking you here," Tanner said.

"Listen," R. L. Davis began to say.

Tanner stopped him. "Watch your mouth, boy. I don't listen to you. I don't listen to anybody I don't want to listen to."

R. L. Davis squinted up at him. "I didn't mean it that way. I come here to work for you."

Tanner's gaze dropped slowly from the bent figure down the street to Davis. "Why do you think I'd hire you?"

"You need a gun, I'm your man."

"I didn't see you hit anything the other day."

"Jesus Christ, I wasn't aiming at her. You said yourself just make her jump some."

"Are you telling me what I said?"

"I thought that's what it was."

"Don't think," Tanner said. "Ride out."

"Hell, you can always use another man, can't you?"

"Maybe a man," Tanner said. "Ride out."

"Try me out. Put me on for a month."

"We'll put some poles on your back," Tanner said, "if you want to stay here."

"I was just asking," R. L. Davis lifted his reins and flicked them against the neck of his sorrel, bringing the animal around and guiding it through the group of riders, trying to take his time.

Tanner watched Davis until he was beyond the pump and heading down the street. The small stooped figure was now at the far end of the adobes.

The woman, Gay Erin, who had been married to the sutler at Fort Huachuca and had been living with Frank Tanner since her husband's death, waited for Tanner to turn and notice her in the doorway behind him. But he didn't turn; he stood on the edge of the platform over his men.

She said, "Frank?" and waited again.

Now he looked around and came over to her, taking his time. "I didn't know you were there," he said.

She kept her eyes on him, waiting for him to come close. "I don't understand you," she said.

"I don't need that boy. Why should I hire him?"

"The other one. He asks you a simple thing, to help someone."

"We won't talk about it out here," Tanner said. They

went into the dimness of the warehouse, past sacks of grain and stacked wooden cases, Tanner holding her arm and guiding her to the stairway. "I let you talk to me the way you want," Tanner said, "but not in front of my men."

Upstairs, in the office that had been made into a sitting room, Gay Erin looked out the window. She could see R. L. Davis at the end of the street; the hunched figure of Bob Valdez was no longer in sight.

"You better keep up here from now on," Tanner said, "unless I call you down."

She turned from the window. "And how long is that?"

"I guess as long as I want." Tanner went into the bedroom. He came out wearing his coat, strapping on a gunbelt. "I'm going to Nogales; I'll be back in the morning." He looked down at his belt, buckling it. "You can come if you want a twenty-mile ride."

"Or sit here," the girl said.

He looked up at her. "What else?"

"If you say sit I'm supposed to sit." Her expression and the sound of her voice were mild, but her eyes held his and hung on. "No one can be that sure," she said. "Not even you."

"Well, you're not going to leave," Tanner said. He moved toward her, settling the gunbelt on his hips. "You don't have anything at Huachuca. You don't have anything left at Prescott. Whatever you have is here."

"Whatever I have," the girl said, "as your woman."

"Aren't I nice enough to you?"

"Sometimes."

"Take what you get."

"Sometimes you act like a human being."

"When I'm in my drawers," Tanner said. "When I'm in my boots that's a different time."

"You had them on outside."

"You bet I did, lady."

"He was trying to help a woman who'd lost her husband; that's all he was doing."

"And I'm helping one already," Tanner said. "One poor widow woman's enough." He was close to her, looking into her face, and he touched her cheek gently with his hand. He said, "I guess I could stay a few more minutes if you like."

"Frank, send someone to cut him loose."

Tanner shook his head, tired of it. "Lady, you sure can break the spell . . ." He moved away from her toward the door, then looked back as he opened it. "Nobody cuts him loose. I don't want to see that man again."

You've looked at the ground all your life, Valdez thought at one point. But never this close for so long.

The pain reached from the back of his neck down into his shoulders. He would try to arch his back, and the pole, with a knot in it, would press against his head and push his hat forward. The hat was low and stuck to his forehead and sweat stung his eyes. He told himself, The hell with it; don't think about it. Go home. You've walked home before.

God, but he had never walked home like this. The ground across the grazing land was humped and spotted with brush, but he had little trouble with his footing. No, God, he could see where he was going all right. He could hear Tanner's cattle and he thought once, What if some bull with swords on his head sees you and doesn't like you? God, he said to himself, give that bull good grass to eat or a nice cow to do something with.

A mile across the grazing land and then up into the foothills, following a gully and angling out of it, climbing the side of a brush slope, not finding the trail and taking a longer way to the top, trying to look up to see where he was going with the pole pressed against his head. He couldn't go straight up. He couldn't lose his footing and fall backward on the crossed poles. He remembered what the segundo had said about the turtle, and at that time he had pictured himself lying on his back in the sun of midday and through the afternoon. No, he would take longer and he wouldn't fall. It was the pain in his legs that bothered him now; it turned his thighs into cords and pulled so, as he neared the top, that his legs began to tremble.

They're old legs, he said to himself. Be good to them. They have to walk twenty miles. Or over to Diego Luz, he thought then. Ten miles. Twenty miles, ten miles, what was the difference?

He wished he could wipe the sweat and dust from his face. He wished he could loosen his hat and rub his nose and bring his arms down and straighten up just for a minute.

Before he reached the crest of the slope he crouched forward and gradually lowered himself to his knees, bending over and twisting his body as he fell forward so that a tip of the crosspole touched the slope first; but this did little to break his fall, and with his head turned his cheekbone struck the ground with the force of a heavy, solid blow. It stunned him and he lay breathing with his mouth open. His hat, tight to his forehead, had remained on; good. Now he rested for perhaps a quarter of an hour, until the pain through his shoulder blades became unbearable. Valdez got to his feet and continued on.

R. L. Davis waited for him in the trees, across the meadow on the far side of the slope. He had watched Valdez work up through the ravine and down the switchback trail on this side. He had waited because maybe Tanner's men were also watching—the lookouts up on the slope—and he had waited because he wasn't sure what they'd do. He thought they might come out and push Valdez down the trail, have some fun with him; but no one appeared, and Valdez had come all the way down to the meadow now and was coming across, hurrying some as he saw the shade of the trees waiting for him.

R. L. Davis moved his sorrel into heavy foliage. There wasn't any hurry: watch him a while and then play with him.

Goddam, now what was he doing, kicking at the leaves? Clearing a spot, R. L. Davis decided. He could hear Valdez in the silence, the sound of the leaves scuffing, and could see him through the pale birch trunks, the bent-over hunched-back figure in the thin shafts of sunlight. He watched Valdez go to his knees; he winced and then smiled as Valdez fell forward on the side of his face. That was pretty good. But as Valdez lay there not moving, R. L. Davis became rest-

less and started to fidget and tried to think of something. You could trample him some, he thought. Ride
over him a few times. He decided maybe that was the
thing to do and raised his reins to flick the sorrel.

But now the man was stirring, arching onto his head
and getting his knees under him.

Valdez rose and stood there, trying to turn his head
to look about him. He moved forward slowly, shuffling
in the leaves. He turned sideways to edge between
trees that grew close together. Farther on he stopped
and placed one end of the crosspole against a birch
tunk and waved the other end of the pole toward a tree
several feet from him, but the pole was too short. R. L.
Davis watched him move on, touching a trunk and trying to reach another with the crosspole until finally
there it was, and R. L. Davis saw what he was trying to
do.

Valdez stood between two trees that were a little less
than six feet apart. Now, with the ends of the crosspole
planted against the trunks, holding him there, he tried
to move forward, straining, digging in with his boots
and slipping in the leaves. He bent his wrists so that
his hands hung down and were out of the way. Now he
moved back several steps and ran between the two
trees. The ends of the crosspole struck the trunks and
stopped him dead. He strained against the pole, stepping back and slamming the pole ends against the
trunks again and again. Finally he moved back eight or
ten feet and again ran at the space between the trees
and this time as the ends struck, R. L. Davis heard a
gasp of breath in the silence.

He moved the sorrel out of the foliage. Valdez must

hear him, but the man didn't move; he hung there on the crosspole leaning against the trunks, his arms seeming lower than they were before.

R. L. Davis saw why as he got closer. Sure enough, the pole had splintered. And it looked like a sharp end had pierced his back. R. L. Davis sat in his saddle looking down at the blood spreading over Valdez's back. He reined the sorrel around the near birch tree and came up in front of him.

"I swear," R. L. Davis said, "you are sure one dumb son of a bitch, aren't you? When that pole broke, where did you suppose it was going to go?" He saw Valdez try to raise his head. "It's your old amigo you tried to swing a scatter gun at the other day. You remember that? You went and shot the wrong coon and you was going to come at me for it."

Davis sidestepped the sorrel closer to Valdez, pulling his coiled *reata* loose from the saddle thong and playing out several feet of it. He reached over, looping the vertical pole above Valdez's head and snugged the knot tight. "You're lucky a white man come along," Davis said.

Valdez tried to raise his eyes to him. "Look at my back," he said.

"I saw it. You cut yourself."

"God, I think so," Valdez said. "Cut my wrists loose first, all right?"

"Well, not right yet," Davis said. He moved away, letting out rope, and when he was ten feet away dallied the line to his saddle horn. "Come on," he said.

Valdez had to move to the side to free an end of the crosspole and was almost jerked from his feet, stumbling to get between the trees and keep up with the short length of rope. He was pulled this way, through the birch trees and through the brush that grew along the edge of the grove, and out into the glare of the meadow again.

"You must ache some from stooping over," R. L. Davis said.

"Cut my hands and I'll tell you about it."

"You know I didn't like you trying to hit me with that scatter gun."

"I won't do it anymore," Valdez said. "How's that?"

"It made me sore, I'll tell you."

"Cut me loose and tell me, all right?"

R. L. Davis moved in close in front and lifted the loop from the upright pole. He kept the sorrel close against Valdez as he coiled the rope and thonged it to his saddle again.

"Your animal doesn't smell so good," Valdez said.

"Well, I'll give you some air," R. L. Davis said. "How'll that be?" He moved the sorrel tight against Valdez, kicking the horse's left flank to sidestep it and keep it moving.

Valdez said, "You crazy, you put me over. Hey!" He could feel the bottom of the upright pole pushing into the ground, wedged tight, and his body lifting against R. L. Davis' leg. The sorrel jumped forward, sidestepping, swinging its rump hard against Valdez, and he went over, seeing Davis above him and seeing the sky and tensing and holding the scream inside him and gasping as his spine slammed the ground and the splintered pole gouged into his back.

After a moment he opened his eyes. His hat was off.

It was good, the tight band gone from his forehead. But he had to close his eyes again because of the glare and the pain in his body, the sharp thing sticking into his back that made him strain to arch his shoulders. A shadow fell over him and he opened his eyes to see R. L. Davis far above him on the sorrel, the funneled hat brim and narrow face staring down at him.

"A man ought to wear his hat in the sun," R. L. Davis said.

Valdez closed his eyes and in a moment the sun's glare pressed down on his eyelids again. He heard the horse break into a gallop that soon faded to nothing.

FOUR

●

St. Francis of Assisi was the kindest man
who ever lived. Maybe not kinder than Our
Lord; that was different. But kinder than
any real living man. Sure. St. Francis had
been a soldier once and got wounded and
after that he wouldn't step on bugs or kill
animals. Hell, he talked to the animals; like
the time he talked to the wolf—probably a
big gray lobo—who was scaring everybody
and he told the wolf to stop it. Stop it or I'll
skin you, you son of a bitch, and wear you
for a coat. You would talk to a wolf different
than you would talk to other animals. But
he talked to all of them, birds, everything;
they were all his friends he said. He even
talked to the stars and the sun and the
moon. He called the sun Brother Sun.

But not today you couldn't call it Brother
Sun, Bob Valdez thought.

It was strange the things he thought
about, lying in the meadow on a pole like a
man crucified, remembering his older sister
reading to him a long time ago about St.

Francis of Assisi and his prayer, or whatever it was, The Canticle of the Sun. Yes, because he had pictured the sun moving, spinning and doing things, the sun smiling, as his sister read it to him. Today the sun filled the sky and had no edges. It wasn't smiling; this day the sun was everything over him, white hot pressing down on him and dancing orange, red, and black dots on his closed eyelids.

He remembered a man who had no eyelids, who had been staked out in the sun and his eyelids cut off. And his ears cut off also and his right hand. He remembered finding the man's hand and finding the man's son in the burned-out farmhouse on the Gila River south of San Carlos, after Geronimo had jumped the reservation and raided down into old Mexico. They didn't find the man's wife. No, he didn't remember a woman there. Maybe she had been away visiting relatives. Or they had taken her. No, they had been moving fast and she wouldn't have been able to keep up with them. It was funny, he wondered what the woman looked like.

She could look like the Lipan Apache woman and have a child inside her. She could look like the woman with Tanner standing on the loading platform—he remembered her blond hair and her eyes watching him, a blond-haired woman in that village of guns and horses and freight wagons. Her face was brown and she looked good with the sun on her hair, but she should be inside in a room with furniture and gold statue lamps on the tables.

He remembered the girl Polly at Inez's place and her robe coming open as she leaned over to look at the green book and then the black one. He should have stayed. It would be good to be there. It didn't matter about the girl—later—but to be in a bed with the shades down, lying on one side and then the other and moving his arms, bending them all he wanted while he slept. He would only wake up at night when the sun was down and Brother Moon or Sister Moon or whatever the hell St. Francis called it was in the sky with its soft light, and he would drink cool water from the pitcher next to the bed. When the girl came in he would turn his head and see her face, her eyes in the darkness, close to him. She had dark hair, but he thought of her with light hair, and this didn't make sense to him.

He remembered turning his head against the thong holding him to the upright post, the thong cutting his neck as he strained to twist his face away from the white heat pressing him and the colors dancing in his eyes. He remembered thinking that if the thong was wet with his sweat it would shrink when it dried and perhaps strangle him to death if he was still alive. Then he wouldn't be thirsty anymore and it wouldn't matter if his eyes were burned out. It wouldn't matter if Brother Wolf came to see him; he wouldn't have to talk to any Brother Wolf and ask him to go away.

He remembered the knife pain in his shoulders and back. He remembered feeling sick and trying to calm himself and breathe slowly so he wouldn't vomit and drown in his own bile in a mountain meadow. He remembered the worst, the heat and the pain and the thirst, and he remembered opening his eyes to a blue sky turning gray and streaked with red. He remembered a numbness in his body, looking at his hands and unable to move them.

He remembered darkness, opening his eyes and seeing darkness and hearing night sounds coming from the birch trees. He remembered the breeze moving the grass close to his face. He remembered pieces of the whole, sleeping and opening his eyes: the girl from Inez's place over him, lifting his head and holding a canteen to his lips. Why would she use a canteen when the pitcher was on the table? He remembered getting up, standing and falling and the girl holding his arms, bending them carefully, working the joints and feeling a sweet pain that would have made his eyes water if he had water left in him to come out. He remembered stretching and walking and falling and walking and crawling on his hands and knees. He remembered voices, the voices of children and a voice that he knew well and an arm that he knew helping him.

Diego Luz said, "Are you awake?"

Valdez lay with his eyes open, his eyes moving slowly from the ceiling of the room to Diego Luz, a white figure in the dimness. "I think so," he said. "I woke up before, I think; but I didn't know where I was."

"You were saying some crazy things."

"How did you find me?"

"Find you? You crawled into the yard last night. I heard the dogs; I almost shot you."

"I came here myself?"

Diego Luz moved closer to the bed. "What happened to you?"

"Maybe I'm dead," Valdez said. "Am I dead?" He

could see the children of Diego Luz behind their father, in the doorway.

"You looked near to it. Somebody stabbed you in the back."

"No, a tree did that."

Diego Luz nodded. "A tree. What kind of a tree is it does that?"

His daughter came into the room with a gourd and a tin cup, and the small children followed her, crowding up to the bed. Valdez smiled at them and at the girl and got up on his elbow to sip the water. He could see the wife of Diego Luz and his wife's mother in the doorway, staying in the other room but raising their faces to look at him on the bed.

"I don't see your boy," Valdez said.

"He's watching."

"For what?"

"To see if they follow you. Or whoever it was."

"Don't worry," Valdez said. "I'm leaving when I find my pants."

"I don't worry," the horsebreaker said. "I'm careful. I wonder when I see a man crawl in half dead."

Valdez handed the cup to the girl. "Have you got some whiskey?"

"Mescal."

"Mescal then."

"You haven't eaten yet."

"I want to sleep, not eat," Valdez said. "In the back of your wagon when you take me to Lanoria."

"Stay here, you be better."

"No," Valdez said. "You said they come by here. Maybe they come by again."

"Maybe they know where you live too."

"I'm not going where I live." He motioned Diego Luz closer and whispered to him as his children and his wife and his wife's mother watched.

Diego Luz straightened, shaking his head. "Half dead and you want to go to that place."

"Half alive," Valdez said. "There is a difference."

Diego Luz brought him in through the kitchen at almost four in the morning. Valdez had passed out in the wagon, his wound beginning to bleed again. But as they dragged him up the stairs and along the dark hallway, Diego Luz and the large woman, Inez, supporting him between them, he hissed at them, "God*dam*, put my arms down!"

"We carry you and you swear at us," Inez hissed back.

"God and St. Francis, put me down!"

"Now he prays," Inez said. She opened a door, and inside they lowered him gently to the bed, settling him on his stomach and hearing him let out his breath. Inez bent over him, lifting his shirt to look at the bloodstained bandage.

"In the back," she said. "The only way you could kill this one." She looked at Diego Luz. "Who shot him? I didn't hear anything."

"A tree," Diego Luz said. "Listen, get something to clean him and talk after."

Valdez heard the woman close the door. He was comfortable and he knew he would be asleep again in a moment. He said, "Hey," bringing Diego Luz close

to the side of the bed. "I'm going to leave you everything I have when I die."

"You're not going to die. You got a little cut."

"I know I'm not going to die now. I mean when I
die."

"Don't talk about it," Diego Luz said.

"I leave you everything I have if you do one more
thing for me, all right?"

"Go to sleep," Diego Luz said, "and shut up for a
while."

"If you get me something from my room at the
boarding house."

"You want me to go now?"

"No, this time of night that old lady'll shoot you.
During the day. Tomorrow."

"What is it you want?"

"In the bottom drawer of the dresser," Valdez said.
"Everything that's there."

Goddam, he wished he could tell somebody about it.
R. L. Davis stood at the bar in the Republic Hotel
drinking whiskey. He didn't have anything to do. He'd
been fired for not being where he was supposed to be,
riding fence and not riding all over the goddam country, Mr. Malson had said. He'd told Mr. Malson he'd
gone to see Diego Luz about a new horse, but Mr. Malson didn't believe him, the tight-butt son of a bitch.
Sure he had gone off to Tanner's place to see about
working for him, figuring the chance of getting caught
and fired was worth it. What surprised him was Tanner not hiring him. Christ, he could shoot. Probably
good or better than any man Tanner had. He saw him-

self riding along with Tanner's bunch, riding into Lanoria, stampeding in and swinging down in front of
the Republic or De Spain's.

He could go over to De Spain's. At least he'd been
paid off. Maybe there was somebody over there he
could tell. God, it was hard to keep something that
good inside you. But he wasn't sure how everybody
would take it, telling how he'd pushed Valdez over like
a goddam turtle in the sun. The segundo had mentioned the turtle and it had given him the idea, though
he thought one of Tanner's men would do it first.

Maybe if he told Tanner what he did——

No, Tanner would look at him and say, "You come
all the way out here to tell me that?"

He was a hard man to talk to. He looked right
through you without any expression. But it would be
something to ride for him, down into old Mexico with
guns and beef and shoot up the federals.

R. L. Davis finished his whiskey and had another
and said to himself all right, he'd go over to De
Spain's. Maybe there was a way of telling it that it
wouldn't sound like he'd done it to him deliberately.
Hell, he hadn't killed him, he'd pushed him over, and
there were seven hundred miles between pushing and
killing. If the son of a bitch was still out there it was his
own fault.

Outside, he mounted the sorrel and moved up the
street. He came to the corner and looked around, seeing who was about, not for any reason, just looking.
He saw Diego Luz coming out of the boardinghouse
two doors from the corner: Diego Luz coming toward
him, carrying something wrapped up in newspaper, a

big bundle that could be his wash. Except a Mexican horsebreaker wasn't going to have any wash done in there. He had his own woman for that.

He waited for him to reach the corner. "Hey, Diego, what you got there, your laundry?"

The Mexican looked funny, surprised, like he'd been caught stealing chickens. Then he gave a big smile and waved, like R. L. Davis was his best friend and he was really glad to see him.

Dumb Mexican. He was all right; just a dumb chilipicker. Christ, R. L. Davis thought, it'd be good to tell him what he'd done to Bob Valdez. And then he thought, Hey, that's the boardinghouse Bob Valdez lives in, isn't it?

Each of the seven doors in the upstairs hall bore the name of a girl in a flowery pink and blue scroll—Anastacia, Rosaria, Evita, Elisaida, Maria, Tranquiliña, and Edith. The names were a nice touch and Inez liked them, though only one of the original seven girls was still here. Because of the turnover during the past two years, and because the Mexican sign painter had moved away, Inez had not bothered to have the doors relettered. Maybe she would sometime, though none of her customers seemed to mind that the name on the door didn't match the girl. They didn't care what the girls' names were, long as they were there.

Inez tiptoed down the hall, but the floor still creaked beneath her weight. It was semidark, with one lamp lit at the end of the hall and a faint light coming from the stairway landing. Polly followed her, carrying a tray of ham and greens and fried potatoes and coffee: Bob

Valdez's supper if he was awake and felt like eating. He had been here since yesterday morning: two days and going on the second night, sleeping most of the time and sitting up drinking water out of the pitcher when he wasn't sleeping. She had never seen a man drink so much water. Diego Luz had come yesterday afternoon with a bundle of clothes—at least what looked to be clothing—and hadn't been back since then. Diego Luz never came here ordinarily, unless he was looking for someone for Mr. Malson, so it would seem strange if he were seen coming in and out. This was why Bob Valdez told him to stay away. No one was to know he was here. "As far as anybody thinks, I have disappeared," Bob Valdez had said. He had told Inez what happened to him, but she had the feeling he didn't tell her everything. That was all right; it was his business. He told what he wanted, but he always told the truth.

At Rosaria's door Inez paused, listening, taking a key from the folds of her skirt. She turned it in the lock and opened the door quietly, in case he was asleep.

She was surprised to see light from the overhead lamp; she was even more surprised to see Bob Valdez standing by the dresser. She got Polly into the room and locked the door and saw the look on Polly's face as she stared at Bob Valdez.

"Put it down," Inez said. "Before you drop it."

"Over here," Valdez said. "If you will."

Crossing the room, Polly kept her eyes on him as he moved aside the newspaper and oil can and revolver so she could place the tray on the dresser. He was holding his sawed-off ten-bore Remington shotgun, wiping it with a cloth that two days before had been his shirt.

Inez smiled a little watching him, noticing the shot-gun shells now on the dresser, the shells standing up-right with their crimped ends peeled open. "Roberto Valdez returned," she said.

He smiled back at her. "Bob is easier."

"Bob wears a starched collar," Inez said. "Roberto makes war."

"Just a little war, if he wants it," Valdez said.

"You get crazier every day."

"I ask him once more; that's all."

"You've asked him twice."

"But this time will be different."

"You expect to fight him?"

"If he wants a little. We'll see."

"*We*. There's one of you."

"The ham smells good. Potatoes, fresh vegetables." He smiled at Polly, then moved his gaze back to Inez. "You got any beef tallow?"

"I'll look," Inez said. "Or maybe you can use ham fat."

"I cut lean slices specially," Polly said. She was frowning, trying to understand why a man would want beef tallow when he had a plate of baked ham in front of him.

"He doesn't want it to eat," Inez said, watching Valdez. "He puts the tallow in the shotgun shell; it holds the charge together so it doesn't fly all over the place. How far would you say, Roberto?"

Bob Valdez shrugged. "Maybe a hundred and fifty feet."

"Boom, like a cannon," Inez said. "His own army. Listen, we'll give you food to take, whatever you want."

"I'm grateful."

"When are you going?"

"When Diego brings the horse."

"You're not taking him, are you?"

"No. One is as good as two."

"But not as good as two dozen."

"Maybe a little whiskey with the coffee, if you got some."

"And some to take for your nerve," Inez said. "When do you plan to be back?"

"Two days, three. I don't know."

"So if you're not back in three days——" Inez said.

Valdez smiled. "Pray for me."

A little while later they watched him leave to begin his war: the Valdez from another time, the Valdez in leather *chivarra* pants and the long-barreled Walker Colt on his right thigh, carrying his shotgun and a Sharps carbine and field glasses and a big canteen and a warbag for the ham and biscuits, the Valdez no one had seen in ten years.

He reached the birch forest before dawn, dismounting and leading his buckskin gelding through the gray shapes of the trees to the far side, to the edge of the meadow that reached to the slope where Tanner's lookouts were stationed. The night was clear and there was no sign of life on the hill. But they would be there, he was sure; how many, he would have to wait and see.

In the first light he moved along the edge of the thicket to the place where R. L. Davis had crowded his horse against him and pushed him over. Valdez did not leave the cover of the trees; he could see the cruciformed poles lying in the open; he could see, at the ends of the crosspole and in the middle, the leather thongs that had been cut by someone in the darkness, a shape close to him, an arm raising his head to give him water, hands helping him to his feet. He must have been out of his head not to remember; he must have been worse off than he imagined. Three days ago he had been lying here in the sun. Already it seemed as if it had happened in another time, years before. He moved back to a place where he would have a good view of the slopes across the meadow, and here he dropped his gear and settled down to wait, propping his field glasses on his warbag and canteen and lying behind them to hold his gaze on the slope.

About six o'clock, not quite an hour after first light, three riders appeared against the sky at the top of the slope. They came down into the deep shadows, and shortly after, a single rider passed over the crest going the other way. One at night, Valdez marked down in his mind, and three during the day. Though maybe not all day.

But it did turn out to be all day. Valdez remained in the thicket watching the slope, seeing very little move-ment; no one came down the trail or crossed the meadow toward the slope; the lookouts remained in dense brush most of the time, and if he did not know where to look for them through the glasses, he proba-bly wouldn't have noticed them. At about five o'clock in the evening a rider came over the crest of the ridge, and soon after the three lookouts climbed the switchbacks and disappeared.

There you are, Valdez said to himself. How do you like it now? It doesn't get any better.

He had not eaten all day and had taken only a few sips of water. Now he ate some of the ham and biscuits and a handful of red peppers; he took a sip of the whiskey Inez had given him and a good drink from the canteen. Valdez was ready.

Crossing the meadow, he let his hand fall to the Walker Colt and eased the barrel in its holster. The stock of the Sharps carbine rested against the inside of his left knee, in the saddle boot; the sawed-off Remington hung on the right side, looped to the saddle horn by a short length of suspender strap. By now the lookout would have seen him and studied him and would be ready. Three of them yesterday came down to meet R. L. Davis, but one up there now would stay put and plan to take him by surprise. Valdez let the buckskin walk, but nudged his heels into its flanks as they reached the rocks and brush and started up the trail.

Now it comes, Valdez thought. When he's ready. Any time. He let himself slouch in the saddle, his shoulders moving with the gait of the horse, a rider climbing a trail, a man relaxed and off guard, in no hurry. Surprise me, he said in his mind to the lookout. I'm nothing to be afraid of. Come out in the open and stop me. I could be one of your friends.

He was a little more than halfway up the slope when the rider appeared, fifty yards and three switchback levels above him. Valdez pretended not to see him and came on, rounding a switchback and reaching an almost level stretch of the trail before the man called out in Spanish, "Enough!"

The Mexican. Valdez recognized the voice and, as he looked up now, the shape of the man on his horse—brown man and brown horse against the evening shadows of the brush slope. The Mexican came down the trail toward him, stopping and coming on again, the sound of his horse's hooves clear in the stillness, reaching the level above Valdez, then tight-reining, his horse moving loose shale as he came down to the stretch of trail where Bob Valdez waited. The Mexican stopped about fifty feet away, facing him on the narrow ledge of the path.

"I thought it was you, but I said no, that man carries a cross on his back."

"I got tired of it," Valdez said.

"Somebody found you, uh?"

"Somebody."

"You had luck with you that time."

"If people help you," Valdez said, "you don't need luck."

"That's it, uh? I didn't know that."

"Sure, like you and me," Valdez said. "We can be friends if we want. We talk awhile. I give you a drink of whiskey. What do you think about something like that?"

"I think I see a lot of guns," the Mexican said. "You come up here to talk and you bring all those guns?" He was at ease, smiling now.

"This little thing?" Valdez raised the cutoff Remington in his right hand, his fingers around the neck of the stock, the stubby barrels pointing straight up. "You think this could hurt somebody? It's for rabbits."

"For rabbits," the Mexican said, nodding. "Sure, there are plenty of rabbits around here. That's what you come for, uh, to hunt rabbits?"

"If I see any maybe. No, I come to ask you to do something for me."

"Because we're good friends," the Mexican said.

"That's right. As a friend I want you to go see Mr. Tanner and tell him Valdez is coming."

The Mexican was silent for a moment, his head nodding slightly as he studied Valdez and thought about him. "You come to see me," the Mexican said then. "How do you know I'm here?"

"You or somebody else," Valdez said. "It doesn't matter."

"You mean me *and* somebody else. Somebody over in the rocks behind you."

"I'll tell you something," Valdez said. "I've been here all day. I saw three of you come and one of you leave. I saw one of you come and three of you leave. There's no somebody else in the rocks—there's just you in front of me. That's all."

The Mexican watched him, unmoving. "You're certain of that? You'd bet your life on it?"

"It's on the table," Valdez said.

The Mexican grinned. "What is this kind of talk with two friends? You want me to go tell him something? All right, I tell him. Put the rabbit gun down." He lifted his reins and began sidestepping his horse to turn around on the narrow trail. Looking at Valdez again, he said, "You wait here, all right? I go tell him what

you say and then I come back and tell you what he say.
How is that?"

Valdez nodded. "I'll be here." He lowered the shotgun, resting it across his lap.

"Sure, stay right there. It don't take me any time."

The Mexican turned in his saddle and started away,
his back to Valdez until he reached the end of the ledge
and kicked his horse up over the shale at the switchback, and now, on the level above Valdez and seventy
or eighty feet away, came back toward him.

Valdez's right thumb eased back both hammers, his
finger curled inside the guard and felt the tension of
the first trigger. The Mexican was spurring his horse
now, kicking it to a gallop up the low angle of the trail,
holding the reins in his left hand. Valdez saw nothing
but the Mexican coming and it was in his mind that the
man would go past him and suddenly turn and fire
from behind. But thirty feet away closing to twenty, he
saw the Mexican's right hand come up with the revolver and there it was, right now, the Mexican
hunched low in the saddle, screaming *Aiiiii* for the
horse or for himself, the revolver across the horse's
mane, the man offering only his left leg and side and
shoulder, but it was enough. Valdez brought up the
barrels of the Remington from his lap, and with the
ten-bore explosion close in front of him, the Mexican
came out of his saddle, flung back over the horse's
rump, his revolver discharging as he struck the
ground, and the buckskin beneath Valdez throwing its
head and trying to dance away from the man, and
loose shale coming down the slope at them. The Mexican rolled to his back almost beneath the buckskin, his

clothes filmed with fine dust, a dark, wet stain spreading from his side down over his thigh. His eyes were open and he had his left arm tight to his side.

"How do you feel?" Valdez asked.

The Mexican said nothing, staring up at him with a dazed expression.

Valdez dismounted and went to his knees over the man, raising his arm gently to look at the wound. The shotgun charge had torn through his side at the waist, ripping away his belt and part of his shirt and leather chaps.

"You should have this taken care of," Valdez said. "You know somebody can sew you up?"

The Mexican's eyes were glazed, wet looking. "What do you put in that thing?"

"I told you, something for rabbits. Listen, I'm going to get your horse and put you on it."

"I can't ride anywhere."

"Sure you can." Valdez lowered the Mexican's arm and gave his shoulder a pat. The Mexican winced and Valdez smiled. "You ride to Mr. Tanner, all right? Tell him Valdez is coming. You hear what I said? Valdez is coming. But listen, friend, I think you better go there quick."

FIVE

●

"**H**e's dying," the segundo said. "Maybe before tonight."

The Mexican was on his back at the edge of the loading platform where they had taken him off his horse and laid him on his back. His eyes looked up at the segundo and at Frank Tanner standing over him. He could hear the people in the street, but he did not have the strength or the desire to turn his head to look at them. He heard the segundo say he was dying and he knew he was dying, now, as the sun went down. He was thinking, I should have gone past him and turned and shot him. Or I should have shot him as he came up, before he saw me. Or I could have gone higher and used the rifle. He wished he could begin it again, do it over from the time Valdez started up the trail, but it was too late. He could see Valdez raising the gun, the blunt double barrels looking at him; he could see Mr. Tanner looking at him, the mouth beneath the moustache barely moving.

"What else did he say?"

The Mexican who was dying stared up at Mr. Tanner, and the segundo said, "Valdez is coming. That's all."

"How do we know it's the same one?"

"It's his name."

"There are a hundred Valdezes."

"Maybe, but it must be the same one," the segundo said. "You said he killed the Negro with a shotgun."

"A farmer gun," Tanner said.

"I don't know," the segundo said. "The way he used it."

Tanner looked up from the Mexican, his gaze lifting beyond the square, beyond the adobes to the ridge of hills in the distance, to the cold red slash of sky above the shadowed slopes. This Valdez killed one of his men up there and said he was coming. For what? It couldn't be to help any dead nigger's Indian woman. He couldn't come in and pull a gun to get money. He'd never get in or out. Then what was he doing? Who was he?

The segundo followed Tanner's gaze to the hills. "He's gone. He wouldn't be there waiting."

"Send somebody and make sure."

"He could be anywhere."

"Well, goddam it, you've got people who read signs?"

"We've got some, sure."

"Then send them," Tanner said. "I want people all over those hills, and if he's there I want him brought in, straight up or face down. I don't care. I want some men sent to Lanoria to look every place he might be and talk to anybody knows him. I want a sign put up on the main street that says Bob Valdez is a dead man and anybody known to be helping him is also dead. You understand me?"

"We start the drive tomorrow," the segundo said.

Tanner looked at him. "We start the drive when I tell you we start it."

The man lying on his back dying, with the wet stain of his blood on the platform now—thinking that this shouldn't have happened to him because of the life in him an hour ago and because of the way he saw himself, aware of himself alive and never thinking of himself dying—looked up at the sky and didn't have to close the light from his eyes. He saw the beard on the segundo's face and the under-brim of his straw hat, and then he didn't see the segundo. He saw Mr. Tanner's face and then he didn't see Mr. Tanner anymore. He saw the open sky above him and that was all there was to see. But the sky wasn't something to look at. If he wasn't on the hill tonight he would be in the adobe that was the cantina, with the oil smoke and the women coming in, lighting a cigar as he looked at them and feeling his belly beneath his gunbelts full of beef and tortillas, bringing a woman close to him and drinking mescal with his hand on the curve of her shoulder, touching her neck and feeling strands of her hair between his fingers. But he had done it the wrong way. He should have looked at the three guns on the man and known something. But he had thought of the man as he had remembered him from before, against the wall and with the cross on his back, and he had listened to the man talk even while he planned to kill the man, being careful not being careful enough, not giving the man enough. He should have thought more about the way the man stood at the wall and watched them shoot at him. He should have remembered the way the man got up with the cross on his back and was kicked down and got up again and walked away. Look —someone should have said to him, or he should have told himself—the man wears three guns and hangs a Remington from his saddle. What kind of man is that? And then he thought, You should know when you're going to die. It should be something in your life you plan. It shouldn't happen but it's happening. He tried to raise his left arm but could not. He had no feeling in his left side, from his chest into his legs. His side was hanging open and draining his life as he looked at the sky. He said to himself, What is the sky to me? He said to himself, What are you doing here alone?

"Ask him if he's sure it's the same one," Tanner said.

The segundo stepped close to the Mexican again. He knew he was dead as he looked at him, though the man's eyes were open, staring at the sky.

The Mexican had reached the village, his head hanging, letting the horse take him, but he seemed to be still alive as he entered the street between the adobes.

You can die any time after you tell them, Valdez had thought, watching through the field glasses at the top of the trail. He had nothing against the man except a kick in the back and the certainty the man had wanted to kill him. He knew the man would die, and it would be better if he did; but he didn't wish the man dead. It would happen, that was all.

Soon they would come out. They would come out in all directions or they would come strung out across the graze toward the trail into the hills. As the Mexican had reached the adobes, Valdez had climbed higher, off the trail now, leading the buckskin up into the rocks. From here he watched the three riders coming first, letting their horses out across the open land. They came up through the ravines and went down the switchbacks on the other side, not stopping. Three more came behind them, but not running their horses, taking their time. They climbed over the trail looking at the ground; coming to the place where Valdez had shot the Mexican they dismounted.

There were others coming out from the village, fanning out, not knowing where they were going. They were nothing. The three looking for his sign were little better than nothing; they had less than an hour of light and no chance of catching up with him. He counted seventeen men who had come out of the village. There would be others with the herd and perhaps others somewhere else. There was no way of knowing how many still in the village. There was no way of knowing if Tanner had come out or was still in the village. He would have to go there to find out. And if Tanner was not in the village he would have to think of another way to do it and come back another time. There was no hurry. It wasn't something that had to be done today or tomorrow or this week. It could be done any time. But you'd better do it tonight, Valdez said to himself, before you think about it too much. Do it or don't do it.

Do it, he thought. He took a sip of the whiskey and

put the bottle back in the warbag that hung from his saddle.

Do it before you get too old.

He took the reins of the buckskin and began working down through the rocks toward the village. He would circle and approach from the trees on the far side, coming up behind the burned-out church.

The clerk from the Republic Hotel, as soon as he was off duty, went over to De Spain's and asked if the three Tanner riders had been there.

Hell, yes, they had. They'd been here and to Bob Valdez's boardinghouse and the Hatch and Hodges office and had stuck their heads into almost every store along the street. They moved fast and didn't waste any questions and you could tell they wanted him bad. Bad? Did you see the sign out in front? Nailed to the post?

It was a square of board, and one of them had lettered on it with charcoal: BOB VALDEZ IS A DEAD MAN. ANYONE HELPING HIM IS ALSO DEAD.

That was how bad they wanted him. They were going to kill him.

If they ever found him. Where the hell was Valdez? Nobody knew. Nobody remembered seeing him in days. The last time was Saturday when he rode out to see Tanner. No, somebody said, he had made the run to St. David the next day. How about since then? Nobody could recall. Maybe he'd been around; maybe he hadn't. Bob Valdez wasn't somebody who stuck in your mind and you remembered.

Mr. Malson said to Mr. Beaudry, "If he's got Tanner

on him and knows it, he'll be seven hundred miles away by now." "Or farther," Mr. Beaudry said. "If he don't know it," somebody said, "then he's a dead man, like the sign says." "There must be something wrong with his head," Mr. Malson said. "Christ, we should have known it the minute he started talking about the Lipan woman something was wrong with him."

R. L. Davis didn't say anything. He wanted to, but he still wasn't sure what people would say. They might say he was crazy. If he'd pushed Valdez over in the sun, then what had he gone back for?

They'd listen to him tell it. "Sure, I pushed him over. I was teaching him a lesson for coming at me with the scatter gun the other day—after he shot the nigger." They'd look at him and say, "You killed a man like that? Like a Indin would do it?"

And he'd say "No, I was teaching him a lesson is all. Hell, I went back and cut him loose and left him a canteen of water." And they'd say "Well, if you cut him loose, where is he?" Somebody else'd say, "If you wanted to kill him, what did you cut him loose for?"

And he'd say, "Hell, if there's something between me and Bob Valdez, we'll settle it with guns. I'm no goddam Apache."

But he had a feeling they wouldn't believe a word of it.

All right, three days ago he'd left Valdez in the meadow. And this evening Tanner's men come in looking for him and write his death sentence. So Valdez must have gone back and done something to them.

Valdez hadn't been here; at least nobody remembered seeing him. So where would he have been the past three days? Not at his boardinghouse.

But, goddam, Diego Luz had been to his boarding-house! He could see Diego again coming out of it and the funny look on the man's face when he realized he'd been spotted.

What would Frank Tanner say about that? R. L. Davis said to himself. If you could hand him Bob Valdez he'd hire you the same minute, wouldn't he?

Go up to Tanner and cock the Walker in his face and say, All right, give me the money, Valdez was thinking. Not asking him, telling him this time. A hundred dollars or five hundred or whatever he had. Take it and get out and don't think about later until later. He would have to leave Lanoria and go someplace else and maybe worry about Tanner the rest of his life—because he had wanted to help the woman; because he had started it and gotten into it and now was so far in he couldn't turn around and walk out. You must be crazy, Valdez thought. Like Inez had said. Or an idiot. But he was here and was going through with it and he wasn't going to think about why he was here.

He was behind the church, bringing the buckskin along close to the wall, then into the alley that led to the yard of the church. At the far end of the yard was the building with the loading platform. Past the low wall of the churchyard he could see the square and the water pump and stone trough. There was no one in the square now. Farther down the street, in the dusk, he could make out people in front of the adobes, a few of the women sitting outside to talk; he could hear voices and laughter, the sound clear in the silence.

Valdez left the buckskin in the yard. He went over the wall and through the narrow space between the platform and two freight wagons that stood ready for loading. He mounted the steps at the far end. On the platform he looked out at the square again and at the church doorway and the fence across the opening. There were a few horses inside; he wondered if one of them was his claybank. Maybe after, he would have time to look. He crossed the platform and went into the building, into the room crowded with wooden cases and sacks of grain. Maybe this wasn't Tanner's place. Maybe he would have to work his way down the street, hurrying before it was full dark and they gave up looking for him. It was already dark in the room. He had to feel his way at first, moving between the cases to the stairway. The boards creaked and his boots on the stairs made a hard, sharp sound that Tanner would hear if he was upstairs; he would be ready or he would think it was one of his men. Valdez reached the hall and opened the door in front of him.

The room was still and seemed empty, until the woman moved and he saw her profile and the soft curve of her hair against the window. She watched him cross the room and open the door to the bedroom, waiting for him to look toward her again.

"He's not here."

Valdez walked toward her. He stopped to look out the window at the square below. "He went with them?"

"I guess he did," the woman said. "He didn't say."

"Are you his wife?"

She didn't answer for a moment, and Valdez looked at her.

"I will be his wife, soon."

"Do you know him?"

"That's a strange question. I guess I know him if I'm going to marry him."

"Well, it's up to you."

There was a silence between them until she said, "Are you going to wait for him?"

"I don't know yet—wait or come back another time."

"He won't give you another time. You killed one of his men."

"He died. I thought he would die," Valdez said. "Unless you had a doctor."

She watched him look out the window again. "Did you come here to kill Frank?"

"It would be up to him," Valdez said.

"Then what do you want?"

"The same thing as before. Something for the woman."

"Why? I mean why do you bother?"

"Listen," Valdez said. He hesitated. "If I tell you what I think, it doesn't sound right. It's something I know. You understand that?"

"Maybe you'll kill him," the woman said, "but you won't get anything out of him."

Valdez nodded slowly. "I've been thinking of that. If he doesn't want to give me anything, how do I make him? I push a gun into him and tell him, but if I have to shoot him, then I don't get anything."

"If he doesn't kill you first," the woman said.

"I've been thinking," Valdez said. "If I have something he wants, then maybe we make a trade. If he wants it bad enough."

She watched him and said nothing. He was looking at her now.

"Like I say to him, 'You give me the money and I give you your woman.'"

She continued to look at him, studying him. "And if he doesn't give you the money?" she said finally.

"Then he doesn't get his woman," Valdez said.

"You'd kill me?"

"No, the question would be how much does he like you?"

"He'll outwait you. He'll put his men around the building and sooner or later you'll have to go out."

"Not if I'm already out," Valdez said. His face went to the window before he looked at her again. "Listen, if you want to take something with you, get it now."

A woman who belonged to one of Tanner's men saw them leave. She had gone to the water pump in the square and stood looking at them as they came out to the loading platform: the woman of Mr. Tanner with a blanket roll and the man carrying a grain pack with something in it and an empty water skin. She looked at them and they looked at her, but she didn't call out. She told Mr. Tanner she was afraid the man would do something to her or to the woman of Mr. Tanner.

"Go on," Tanner said. "Then what?" He was still mounted, standing with his segundo and several of his men in the lantern glow of the square—the lantern on the seat of a freight wagon so Tanner could see the woman while she told what had happened.

"They went to the yard of the church," the woman said to Tanner. Then the man came over the wall toward her and told her to get a horse from the church, asking for a particular claybank horse if it was there. The woman brought out a horse but was not sure of its color in the darkness of the church and it wasn't the claybank but a brown horse. Then he told her to bring a saddle and bridle and a half sack of dried corn.

While this was taking place, the woman of Mr. Tanner was astride a horse in the churchyard, sitting in the saddle as a man does, though she was wearing a dress. "I think a white or a gray dress," the woman said. When Valdez was ready and had mounted the brown horse, he rode into the churchyard and told the woman of Mr. Tanner to follow him.

"Did she say anything to him?" Tanner asked.

"Not that I heard," the woman said.

They left through the alley next to the church. The woman waited until they were in the alley and followed, but by the time she reached the back of the church they were gone.

"Could you hear them?" Tanner asked.

"I think going toward the river," the woman said.

"To reach cover," the segundo said. He was sitting his horse close to Frank Tanner. "Then maybe south into the mountains."

"How long ago?" asked Tanner.

The woman thought about it and said, "Not long.

They would be maybe two or three miles away only. Or a little more if they ran their horses."

"You know what to do," Tanner said to the segundo. "Whoever's here, send them out again."

"In the dark," the segundo said, "how do we see them?"

"You listen," Tanner said. "Somebody could run into them."

The segundo waited, about to speak, but looked at Tanner and then only nodded. It was Tanner's business. No, his business was in the morning with the arms and grain and cattle, taking it all across the border and coming back without being killed. That was his business.

But in the morning the freight wagons stood empty, and Frank Tanner waited on the loading platform for his men to come in. Some of the women stood in the square, watching him, waiting to see what he was going to do. The men came in singly and in small groups and would talk to the segundo while they watered their horses and while the women watched. It was almost midmorning when the three trackers came in. One of them was dead, the other two were wounded.

These three who came along the street single file, one of them facedown over his saddle, were the segundo's best hunters and trackers. They had been in the Army and had lived through the campaigns against the Apache. But now one was dead and another would soon be dead.

Tanner sat in a rocking chair in the morning sunlight and watched them brought in: another dead man on the loading platform and a man coughing blood and a third one, luckier than the first two, shot through the left forearm, the bone shattered, and there was no doubt about that. This one could talk and he told what had happened, his the only voice in the stillness. Tanner listened to the man and did not interrupt. He heard how the three had put themselves in Valdez's place and decided he would follow the river south into the hills of the Santa Ritas, then maybe work his way west around toward Lanoria or maybe not, but they'd take a look.

With the first light this morning they had found tracks, fresh prints of two horses that showed the horses were walking. They weren't sure of this man they were following; he didn't try to keep to rocky ground or cover his tracks, and he walked the horses, maybe thinking he had enough time. Still, when they came to the flat open stretch with the trees in the distance, they were careful, knowing he could be waiting for them in the trees. So they made a plan as they crossed the flat stretch: they would spread out before they got to the cover and come up from three sides and if he was in there they'd have him. But they never got to the trees.

"Listen, it was flat open," the man with the shattered arm said, "out to the sides as far as you could see and a mile in front of us. There was no cover near, hardly any brush to speak of. So it was like he rose up out of the ground behind us. He says, 'Throw down your guns and come around.' This voice out there in the middle of nothing. We stop and come around, keeping our iron though, and there he is standing there. I swear to God there was nothing for him to hide behind, yet we'd come over the ground he was standing on just a moment before.

"He says, 'Go back and tell Mr. Tanner we're waiting for him.' That's what he said, waiting for *him*. Meaning he wasn't talking to anybody else. Then he says, 'Tell Mr. Tanner I got something to trade him.' We looked, but she wasn't anywheres around. Just him, and three of us. I guess we all had it in mind to bust him and he must have saw it. He says again, 'Throw down the guns.' We don't move. He says it again and this time when we don't move he brings up the Colt gun in his right hand and puts one through my arm."

He looked toward the dead man and the man who was lying on the ground shot through the lungs. "They went for theirs with the sound of his piece, and he brings up this little scatter gun in his left hand and lets go both barrels and them two boys take it square. This here boy partly in front of the other, a little closer, and it killed him in his boots.

"Then he says to me, 'You tell him, he wants his woman, come out here with five hundred dollars.'

"I say to him, 'Well, where's Mr. Tanner supposed to come? You going to have signs put up?' And then he points."

The man with the shattered arm, standing by the loading platform, turned half around and raised his right arm, his finger extended; he moved it gradually southwest.

"There, you can see it," the man said, "though it was closer where we were at and you could see it better— twin peaks, the one a little higher than the other. He says for you to point to them and he'll get in touch with you.

"I say to him, 'Well, what if Mr. Tanner don't feel like coming?'

"And he says, standing there with the shotgun and the Colt gun, 'Then I kill his woman.'"

Frank Tanner stared at the twin peaks ten miles in the distance. After a few minutes, when he became aware that he was sitting in a rocking chair on the loading platform and his people were below him in the square, waiting for him to say something, he waved his hand and they cleared out, taking the dead man and the lung-shot man and the man with the shattered left arm, who thought Mr. Tanner might say something to him personally. But he didn't—just the wave of the hand.

The segundo stayed; he was the only one. He waited awhile, getting the words straight in his mind. When he was ready he said, "You go after him, we don't make the trip."

He waited, giving Mr. Tanner a chance to say something, but the only sound was someone working the pump handle, a rattly metal sound in the heat settling over the village.

"We go out there and look for him," the segundo said. "Sure, we find him, but maybe it take us a few days, a week, if he knows what he's doing. We're out there, we're not in Sonora giving the man the things he's paying for. How much is he paying?" The segundo waited again. He said then, "He pay plenty, but nobody pay you to go up in those mountains."

The segundo stood in the sun waiting for Mr. Tanner

to say something. He could stand here all day and this son of a bitch Mr. Tanner might never say anything. The segundo was hot and thirsty. He'd like a nice glass of mescal and some meat and peppers, but he was standing here waiting for this son of a bitch Americano to make up his mind.

So he said, smiling a little, "Hey, what if you don't go out? You let him kill her." His smile broadened and he gestured as if to say, Do you see how simple it is? He said, "Then what? You get another woman."

Frank Tanner, sitting in the rocker, looked at his segundo. He said, "If you were up here I'd bust your face open. And if you wanted any more I'd give you that too. Do you see the way it is?"

The segundo had killed five men in his life that he knew of and had probably killed more if some of them died later or if he wanted to count Apaches. He had hanged a man he caught stealing his horses. He had killed a man with a knife in a cantina. He had shot a man who once worked for him and insulted him and drew his revolver. He had killed two Federales when the soldiers set an ambush to take the goods they were delivering in Sonora. And with others he had wiped out an Apache *ranchería*, shooting or knifing every living person they found, including the old people and the children. But the segundo was also a practical man. He had a wife in this village and two or three more wives in villages south of here, in Sonoita and Naco and Nogales. He had nine children that he knew of. Maybe he had eleven or twelve. Maybe he had fifteen. He had not wanted to kill the Apache children, but they were Apache. He also liked mescal and good

horses and accurate rifles and revolving pistols. He
was number two and Mr. Tanner was number one. He
was thinking, *Shit*. But he smiled at Mr. Tanner and
said, "Why didn't you say so? You want to get this
man, we go get him for you."

Frank Tanner nodded, thinking about the woman.

The time he was in Yuma he thought about women
every day. He'd thought about women before that, but
not the same way he did in that stone prison overlooking the river. He remembered how the men smelled at
Yuma, breaking rocks for twelve hours in the sun,
working on the road, and coming back in to eat the
slop. That's when they'd start talking about women.
Frank Tanner would think, *They don't know a real
woman if they see one*, except for some whore who'd
smile and laugh and give them everything and rot their
insides. No, when he was at Yuma he pictured a blond-
haired girl, real long hair and a pretty face and big
round breasts, though she wouldn't be too big in the
gut or the hips. The hips could be more than a handful,
but she'd have to have a nice sucked-in white gut.
That's the one he pictured at Yuma, after he and Carlisle Baylor got caught with the goddam branded cows
they were running into old Mexico without any bill of
sale. Three years picturing the blond golden-haired
woman. Two years more raising money and buying
stock to sell across the border, buying and selling
horses and cattle and dynamite and about anything he
could lay his hands on they didn't have down there.
He'd bought twenty-five-year-old Confederate muskets
and sold them. He bought a few old Whitworth field
pieces and sold them too. He'd made money and met

people who knew people and pretty soon he was even selling remounts to the United States Cavalry at Fort Huachuca. And that was where he saw the woman, the girl or woman or however you wanted to think of her, there at Huachuca, married to the drunk-ass sutler, who never went a day without a quart of whiskey or a bottle of mescal or even corn beer if he couldn't get any mescal. There she was, the one he'd seen every day at Yuma and about every day since, the blond golden-haired girl who was built for the kind of man he was, sitting in their place talking to the drunk-ass sutler and looking at the woman every chance he got. A year of that; a little more than a year. Talking to her when he wasn't around and trying to find out things about her, about them. Trying to find out if she felt anything for the drunk or not. She felt something when he beat her —sometimes you could see the bruises on her face she couldn't hide with powder—but maybe she liked it. You could never tell about women.

He would have taken her away from the drunk alive, and once he was dead there wasn't anything else to think over. He took her and she came with him. He would marry her, too, but he had things to do and she'd have to wait on that; but in the meantime there wasn't any reason they couldn't live as husband and wife. She saw that and agreed, and she was better than he ever imagined in Yuma she would be. She was real now and she was his, and there wasn't any goddam broken-down Mexican nigger-loving town constable going to run off with her into the hills and threaten to kill her. Valdez, or whatever his name, was a dead man and he could roll over right now and save everybody a lot of time.

Tanner was looking off at the hills that climbed into the Santa Ritas and the twin peaks, far away against the hot sky.

"What's up there?" he said to the segundo.

"Nothing," the segundo answered.

"Why would he want us to track up there?"

"I don't know," the segundo said. "Maybe he's got a place somewhere."

"What kind of place?"

"An Apache camp he's been to," the segundo said. "He knows the Apache—the thing he did to the three of them in the open country, hiding where there's no place to hide."

"He didn't seem like much," Frank Tanner said.

"Maybe," the segundo said. "But he knows the Apache."

R. L. Davis got drunk trying to work up nerve to tell what he did to Bob Valdez and never did tell it. He went over to Inez's, but they wouldn't let him in. Then he didn't remember anything after that. He woke up in the Maricopa bunkhouse when a hand came in and poured water all over him. God, he felt awful. So it was afternoon by the time he got out to Mimbreño.

There seemed to be more activity than the time he was here before, more men in the village sitting around waiting for something, and more horses and more noise. He rode up the street not looking around too much, but not missing anything either. He hoped Mr. Tanner would be outside, and he was, the same place he was the last time, up on the loading platform. The problem was to tell him before Mr. Tanner gave any orders to have him run off or tied to a cross or whatever he might do; so he kept his eyes on Mr. Tanner and the second he saw Mr. Tanner's gaze land on him, R. L. Davis yelled out, "I know where he is!"

They looked at him, all the people standing around there, and let him ride over toward the platform where Mr. Tanner was waiting.

"I think I know where he is," R. L. Davis said to Mr. Tanner.

"You think so or you know so," Tanner said.

"I'd bet a year's wage on it."

"Where?"

"A place up in the mountains."

"I asked you where."

"I was thinking," R. L. Davis said. "Let me ride along and I can show you. Take you right to it."

Tanner kept looking at him deciding something, but showing nothing in his face. Finally he said, "Step down and water your horse."

SIX

Most of the day the woman, Gay Erin, rode behind Valdez as they climbed out of the flatland and across sloping meadows that stretched toward pine timber, in the open sunlight all morning and into the afternoon, until they reached the deep shade of the forest. She noticed that Valdez seldom looked back now. When they had stopped to rest and he stood waiting as the horses grazed, he would look north sometimes, the way they had come, but he stood relaxed and could be looking at nothing more than the view.

Earlier this morning, once it was light, he had looked back. He stopped and looked back for some time as they were crossing flat, open country. When they reached the trees he made her dismount and tied their horses to a dead trunk that had fallen. She watched him walk out of the trees, out across the flats until he was a small figure in the distance. She watched him squat or kneel by a low brush clump and then she didn't see him again, not for more than an hour, not until the three riders appeared and she heard the gunfire. He came back carrying his shotgun; they mounted again and continued on. She asked him, "Did you kill them?" And he answered, "One. Maybe another." She asked, "Why didn't you tie me? I could have run away." He said to her, "Where would you go?"

They spoke little after that. They stopped to rest in a high meadow and she asked him where they were going. "Up there," he answered, nodding toward the rock slopes above them.

Another time she said to him, "Maybe you don't have a natural call to do certain things, but I do." He smiled a little and told her to go ahead, he wouldn't look. She stayed on the off side of her horse and didn't know if he looked or not.

At first she wondered about him, and there were questions she wanted to ask; but she followed him in silence, watching the slope of his shoulders, the easy way he sat his saddle. In time the pain began to creep down her back and into her thighs; she held on to the saddle horn, following the movement of the horse and not thinking or wondering about him after a while, wanting this to be over but knowing he wasn't going to stop until he was ready.

When they reached the edge of the pine timber he dismounted. Gay Erin went to the ground and stretched out on her back in the shade. She could feel her lips cracked and hard and dirt in the corners of her eyes. She wanted water, to drink and to bathe in, but more than water she wanted to stretch the stiffness from her body and sleep.

She heard Valdez say, "We're going to move. Not far, over a little bit." Looking up at the pine branches she closed her eyes and thought, He'll have to drag me or carry me. She could hear him moving in the pine needles and could hear the horses. She waited for him to come over and tell her to get up or kick her or pull her to her feet, but after a while there was no sound, and in the silence she fell asleep.

When she opened her eyes she wasn't sure where she was and wondered if he had moved her. The trees above were a different color now, darker, and she could barely see the sky through the branches. She stretched, feeling the stiffness, and rolled to her side. Valdez was sitting on the ground a few feet away smoking a cigarette, watching her. She pushed herself to a sitting position. "I thought we were moving."

"It's waiting for you," Valdez said.

He led her on foot along the dark-shadowed edge of the timber. Off from them, in the open, dusk was settling over the hills. They walked for several minutes, until she smelled wood burning and saw the horses picketed close below them in the meadow. The camp was just inside the timber, in a cutbank that came down through the pines like a narrow road, widening where it reached the meadow and dropping into the valley below.

At times she looked at him across the low fire, at this man who had taken her up a mountain and let her sleep for a few hours and then served her pan bread and ham and peppers and strong coffee. When they had finished he took a bottle of whiskey from a canvas bag. She watched him now. She could see Jim Erin

with his bottle every evening, saying he was going to
have a couple to relax and pouring a glass and then
another glass, smoking a cigar and taking another
drink, his voice becoming louder as he talked. Sometimes she would go out, visit one of the officers' wives,
and if she could stay long enough he would be asleep
when she got home. But sometimes he wouldn't allow
her to go out and she would have to listen to him as he
pretended he was a man, hearing his complaints and
his obscenities and his words of abuse; the goddam
Army and the goddam fort and the goddam heat and
the goddam woman sitting there with her goddam
nose up in the air. The first time he hit her she doubled
her fist and hit him back, solidly in the mouth, and he
beat her until she was unconscious. For months he
didn't take a drink and was kind to her. But he started
again, gradually, and by the time he had worked up to
his bottle an evening he was slapping her and several
times hit her with his fist. She never fought back after
the first time. She was married to him, a man old
enough to be her father, who perhaps might grow up
one day. Sometimes she thought she loved him; most
of the time she wasn't sure, and there were moments
when she hated him. But he didn't change; he beat her
for the last time and no man would ever beat her
again.

It surprised her when Valdez offered the bottle. "For
the cold," he said. "Or to make you sleep." She hesitated, then took a sip and handed it back to him.
Valdez raised the bottle. When he lowered it he popped
in the cork and got up to put the bottle away.

"I've never seen a man take one drink," she said.

Valdez sat down again by the fire. "Maybe it has to last."

"I was married to a man who drank." He made no comment and she said, "He was killed."

Valdez nodded. "I see."

"What do you see?"

"I mean you were married and now you're not. What's your name?"

"Gay Erin."

He was looking at her but said nothing for a moment. "That's your marriage name?"

"Mrs. James C. Erin."

"Of Fort Huachuca," Valdez said. "Your husband was killed six months ago."

"You knew him?"

He shook his head.

She waited. "Then you heard about it."

Valdez said, "You were in Lanoria Saturday when the man was killed?"

"Frank said an Army deserter was shot."

"No, he wasn't a deserter. Frank Tanner said it was the man that killed your husband, but when he looked at him dead he said no, it was somebody else."

Gay Erin said, "And the Indian woman, the widow——"

"Was the wife of the man we killed by mistake."

She nodded slowly. "I see." She said then, "Frank didn't tell me that."

Valdez watched her. "But you're going to marry him."

"What difference does it make to you?"

"I like to know how much he wants you—if you're worth coming after."

"He'll come," she said.

"I think so too. I think he wants you pretty bad." Valdez placed a stick on the fire and pushed the ends of the sticks that had not burned into the center of the flame. "You know what else I think. I think maybe he wanted you pretty bad when you were still married."

The flame rose to the fresh wood. He could see her face in the light, her eyes holding on his.

"He knew my husband," she said. "Sometimes he'd come to visit. Anyone who was at the hearing knows that."

"And after it you go to live with him."

She was staring at him in the flickering light. "Why don't you say it right out?"

"It's just something I started to wonder."

"You think Frank killed my husband."

"He could do it."

"He could," the woman said, "but he didn't."

"You're sure of that, uh?"

"I know he didn't."

"How do you know?"

"Because I killed him."

She had come from Prescott with her nightgowns and linens to marry James C. Erin, and five years and six months later she fired three bullets into him from a service revolver and left him dead.

Tell this man about it, she thought. The time in the draw at night, a single moment in her life she would see more clearly than anything she had ever experienced. She had told no one about it and now she was telling this man sitting across the low-burning fire, not telling him everything, but not sure what to tell and what to leave out.

She began telling him about Jim Erin and found she had to tell him about her father and the years of living on Army posts and her mother dying of fever when she was a little girl. She remembered Jim Erin when she was younger, in her early teens, and her father was stationed at Whipple Barracks. She remembered Jim Erin and her father drinking together and remembered them stumbling and knocking the dishes from the table. A few years later she remembered her father —after he retired and they were living in Prescott— mentioning Jim Erin and saying he was coming to see them. And when he came she remembered Jim Erin again, the man with the nice smile and the black hair who had a way of holding her arm as he talked to her, his fingers moving, feeling her skin. She remembered her father drinking and cursing the Army and a system that would pass over a man and leave him a lieutenant after sixteen years on frontier station. Now a sutler was something else; he had a government contract to sell stores to the soldiers and could do well. Like his friend Jim Erin. The girl who gets him is getting something, her father had told her, leading up to it, and within a year had arranged the marriage. A year and a half later her father was dead of a stroke.

A lot of men drink, but their wives don't kill them. Of course. It wasn't his drinking. Yes, it was his drinking, but it was more than that. If he wasn't the kind of man he was and he didn't beat her it wouldn't have happened. This was in her mind, though she didn't try to explain it to Valdez. He put wood on the fire, keeping the flame low, while she told him about the night she killed her husband.

It was after Frank Tanner had left. He had come to see Jim Erin on business, with a proposition to supply the sutler's store with leather and straw goods he could bring up from Mexico.

She stared into the fire, remembering that night. "They were drinking when I left to visit for a while," she said. "When I got back Frank was gone and Jim was out of whiskey. He couldn't borrow any. No one would lend it to him, and that night he didn't have enough money to buy any. So he said he was going out to get corn beer . . ."

"He liked tulapai, uh?"

"He liked anything you could drink. He said someone not far away would sell him a bucket of it. I told him he was too drunk to go out alone, and he said then I was coming with him if I was so concerned. Jim got his gun and we took the buggy, not past the main gate, because he didn't want anybody questioning him. There was no stockade and it was easy to slip out if you didn't want to be seen.

"I don't know where we went except it was a few miles from the fort and off the main road. When we finally stopped Jim got out and left me there. He said 'here,' handing me his gun, 'so you won't be scared.' He didn't mean it as kindness; he was saying 'here, woman, I'm going off alone, but I don't need any gun.' Do you see what I mean?"

She looked at Valdez. He nodded and asked her then, "Was he drunk at this time?"

"Fairly. He'd had the bottle with Frank. He stumbled some, weaving, as he walked away from the buggy. There wasn't a house around or a sign of light. He walked off toward a draw you could see because of the brush in it."

"It must have been a half hour before I saw him coming back, hearing him first, because it was so dark that night, then seeing him. He was carrying a gourd in front of him with both hands and when he got to the buggy he raised it and said, 'Here, take it.' He put his foot up on the step plate to rest the gourd on his knee, but as he did it his foot slipped and he dropped the gourd on the rocks. He looked down at the broken pieces and the corn beer soaking into the ground, then up at me and said it was my fault, I should have taken it. He started screaming at me, saying he was going to beat me up good. I said, 'Jim, don't do it. Please,' I remember that. He started to step up into the buggy, reaching for me, and I jumped out the other side. I ran toward the draw, but he got ahead of me, turning me. I said to him, 'Jim, I've got your gun. If you touch me I'll use it.' I remember saying that too. He kept coming, working around me as I faced him, until I was against the side of the draw and couldn't turn. I said to Jim, please. He came at me and I pulled the trigger. Jim fell to his knees, though I wasn't sure I had hit him. He picked up something, I guess a rock, and came at me again, and this time I shot him twice and knew I had killed him."

Valdez rolled a cigarette and leaned into the fire to light it, and raising his eyes he saw the woman staring into the light. She sat unmoving; she was in another time, remembering, her hands folded in her lap. She seemed younger at this moment and smaller, this woman who had killed her husband.

Valdez said, "You didn't tell anyone?"

She shook her head slowly.

"Why didn't you?"

"I don't know. I was afraid. I went back to the post. The next day, after they found him, they asked me questions. I told them Jim had gone out late, but I didn't know where. They told me he was dead and I didn't say anything, because I couldn't pretend to be sorry. When I didn't tell them then, I couldn't tell them later, at the hearing. They decided it must have been the man who deserted, a soldier named Johnson who everybody knew was buying corn beer from the Indians and selling it at the post."

Valdez drew on his cigarette, letting the smoke out slowly. "You haven't told Frank Tanner?"

"No. I almost did. But I thought better of it."

"Then why did you tell me?"

Her eyes raised now in the firelight. "I don't know," she said softly. "Maybe it's this place. Maybe it's because I've wanted to tell somebody so bad. I just don't know." She paused, and with the soft sound gone from her voice said, "Maybe I told you because you're not going to live long enough to tell anyone else."

"You want to stay alive," Valdez said. "Everybody wants to stay alive."

She was staring at him again. "Do you?"

"Everybody," Valdez said.

"Well, remember that when you close your eyes,"

she said. "I killed a man to be free of him, to stay alive."

"I'll remember that," Valdez said. "I'll remember something else, too, a man lying on his back tied to a cross and someone cutting him loose and giving him water."

He watched closely but there was no change of expression on her face. He said, "The man believes a woman did this. He thought the woman had dark hair, because he had been thinking of a woman with dark hair. But maybe he thought it was dark hair because it was night. Maybe it was a woman with light hair. A woman who lived near this place and knew where he was and could find him."

She was listening intently now, hunched forward, her long hair hanging close to her face. She said, "It could have been one of the Mexican women."

"No, it wasn't one of them, I know that. They live with those men and they would be afraid."

She waited, thoughtful, but still did not move her eyes from his. She said, almost cautiously, "You believe I'm the woman?"

"There's no one else."

She said then, still thoughtful, watching him, "If you believe I saved you, why are you doing this to me?"

Valdez took a last draw on the cigarette and dropped it in the fire. "I'm not doing it to you. I'm doing it to Frank Tanner."

"But if he doesn't give you the money——"

"Let's see what happens," Valdez said. He got to his knees and spread his blanket so that his feet would be toward the fire.

Gay Erin didn't move. She said, "Why do you think I cut you loose?"

"I don't know. Because you felt sorry for me?"

"Maybe." She watched him. "Or maybe because of Frank. To do something against him."

"You're going to marry him," Valdez said.

"He says I'm going to marry him."

"Well, if you don't want to, why didn't you leave?"

"Because I've no place to go. So I'll marry him whether I want to or not." She looked into the fire, moving her hair from the side of her face gently, with the tips of her fingers. "I have no family to go to. People I used to know are scattered all over the territory. I think even when I was married to Jim I felt alone. I stayed with him, I guess, for the same reason I'm going to marry Frank."

Valdez knelt on his blanket, half turned to look at her. "You want to get married so bad, there are plenty of men."

"Are there?" She got up and smoothed her skirt, standing close to the fire. "Where should I spread my blanket?"

"Where do you want to?"

Looking down at him she said, "Wherever you tell me."

Look at him again as he looked at himself that night. His name was Roberto Eladio Valdez, born July 23, 1854, in an adobe village on the San Pedro, where the valley land climbed into the Galiuros. His father was a farmer until they moved to Tucson and his father went to work for a freight company and sent his children to the mission school. Roberto Eladio Valdez, born of Mexican parents in the United States Territory of Arizona, a boy who lived in the desert and knew of many people who had been killed by the Apaches, boy to man in the desert and in the mountains, finally working for the Army, leading the Apache trackers when the hostiles jumped San Carlos and went raiding, and finally through with that and deciding it was time to work the land or work for a company, as most men did, and do it now if it wasn't already too late. Roberto Eladio Valdez worked for Hatch and Hodges, and they put him on the boot with the shotgun because he was good with it. He asked the municipal committee of Lanoria for a town job and they made him a part-time constable and put a shotgun in his hands because he was good with it and because he was quiet and because everybody liked him or at least abided him, because he was one of the good ones who kept himself clean and neat, even wearing the starched collar and the suit when everybody else was in shirtsleeves, and never drank too much or was abusive. Remember, there is the Bob Valdez who knew his place, and the one looking for a normal life and a home and a family.

Now this one is inside the one at the high camp above the mountain meadow at the edge of the timber. Bob and Roberto both there, both of them looking at the woman across the firelight, but Roberto doing the thinking now, saying to himself but to the woman, "All right, that's what you want."

He was not smiling now or holding open the coach door or touching his hat and saying yes, ma'am. He was on his own ground and he was unbuckling the Walker Colt from his leg.

He said, "Bring it over here."

He rose to his feet as she came around the fire with the rolled blanket, now taller and bigger than she was. She spread the blanket next to his, and when she straightened, he took her shoulders in his hands, not feeling her pull back, feeling only the soft firmness of her arms. He said, "You don't want to be alone, uh?"

She said nothing.

"You want somebody to hold you and take care of you. Is that it?"

Her face was close, her eyes looking at him, her lips slightly parted.

"What else do you want? You want me to let you go?"

Slowly her hands came up in front of her and she began unbuttoning her shirt, her hands working down gradually from her throat to her waist. She said, "I told you I killed my husband. I told you I don't want to marry Frank Tanner. I told you I have nothing. You decide what I want."

"I heard something," Diego Luz said.

His wife lay beside him with her eyes closed. He knew she was awake because sunlight filtered through the straw blind covering the window, the way the early morning sunlight looked each day when they rose to work in the yard and the fields and the horse corral until the sun left for the night. Without opening her eyes his wife said, sleep in her voice and on her face, "What did you hear?"

Diego Luz sat up now. "I heard something."

"Your horses," his wife said.

"Horses, but not my horses."

"The chickens," she said.

"Horses." Diego Luz got out of the bed Bob Valdez had slept in a few days before. He looked at the two children on the mat beneath the window; they were asleep. He went into the front room and looked at his daughter and his youngest child and his wife's mother in the bed. His mother-in-law lay on her back staring at the ceiling. Diego Luz said, "What is it?"

"Outside," his wife's mother said.

"What outside? What did you hear?"

"They killed the dogs," the old woman said.

He turned to look at his oldest son, sleeping, and said to himself, Wake him. But he let the boy sleep. Diego Luz pushed aside the straw mat covering the doorway and went outside, out under the mesquite-pole ramada, and saw them in the yard.

An army of them, a half-circle of armed men in their saddles. No sound now, not even from the horses. A dozen of them or more. A dog lying on its side in the yard with a saddle blanket covering its head. The dog smothered. Twelve riders looking at him, staring at him or at the ramada or at the house, facing him and not moving. He heard hooves on the hardpack and two riders appeared from the side of the house. Diego Luz looked that way and saw more of them at the corral and coming up from the horse pasture. They were all around the place; they had been everywhere; they had closed in from all sides and now they were here.

Diego Luz moved to the edge of the ramada shade

looking out. He said nothing because there was nothing for him to say; he didn't ask them here; they came. But he said to himself, He did something to them and they're looking for him.

He saw Mr. Tanner and his segundo and several people that he recognized who had been by here. He saw R. L. Davis and this puzzled him, R. L. Davis being with them; but the way they were here, not passing by and stopping for water, *here*, made him too afraid to wonder about R. L. Davis.

Diego Luz, the horsebreaker, who they said broke horses with his fists, looked out at them and said in his mind to them, Go out to the corral and eat horseshit, goddam you sitting there. But he thought of his wife and his children and his oldest daughter and he said, Jesus, son of God, help me. Jesus, if you listen to anything or have listened to anything. Jesus, from now on——

The segundo said in Spanish, "How are you, friend? How is your family? Are they awake?"

Goddam him, Diego Luz thought and said, "How does it pass with you? Come down and have something with us. I'll wake up the old woman."

"Good," the segundo said, "Bring the woman out. Bring out your daughter."

Over from him several riders, R. L. Davis said, "Mr. Tanner you want me to ask him? I'll get it from him."

The segundo looked at R. L. Davis from under the straw brim of his Sonora hat. R. L. Davis saw the look, not moving his eyes to Mr. Tanner, knowing better, and decided to keep his mouth shut for a while.

"Now they come," the segundo said pleasantly, smiling, touching the brim of his hat.

Diego Luz could hear them behind him. He thought, Jesus, make them stay inside. But they were out and coming out: his wife and his son and his daughter, standing close to him now; he could hear one of the smaller children, the high questioning voice, and heard the witch voice of his wife's mother, the too-loud annoying sound telling them to be silent; God bless the toothless hag this time, now, Jesus, give her power to keep them inside.

Diego Luz tried to be calm and let this happen, what was going to happen. He wet his lips and tried not to wet his lips. He did not see the segundo motion or hear him speak, but now a rider dismounted, letting his reins trail, and came toward them.

He was an American, a bony man who had not shaved for several days and wore boots to his knees and spurs that chinged as he came forward. He moved past Diego Luz and took his son by the arm and brought him out several strides into the yard. He positioned the boy, moving him by his shoulders, to face his family as the boy looked up at him. The man glanced at the segundo. His gaze dropped slowly to the boy and when he was looking at him, standing a stride in front of him, he stepped in swinging his gloved right fist and slammed it into the boy's face.

Diego Luz did not move. He looked at his boy on the ground and at the man who had struck him and at the segundo.

The segundo said, "We ask you one time. Where is Valdez?"

Diego Luz did not hesitate or think about it. He said, "I don't know." He added then, "No one here knows." And then, because he had said this much, he said, "He hasn't been here in four days." He saw the segundo looking at him and he wished he had said only that he didn't know.

The American with the bony face and the high boots walked over to the ramada. Diego Luz glanced aside and then half turned as he saw his small children out of the doorway. The American picked up the littlest girl, his three-year-old, and held her up in front of him. The man grinned with no teeth, with his mouth sunken. He said, "How're you, honey?" The little girl smiled as he carried her out into the yard. The American looked out toward the mounted men and he said, "Mr. Tanner, I could swing this young'n by her feet and bash her head agin the wall."

Diego Luz screamed, "I don't know!"

Now several men dismounted and came toward him. One of them pushed him aside and they brought his daughter out into the yard. She was wearing only a nightdress, and in the sunlight he could see the shape of his daughter's hips and legs beneath the cotton cloth and saw the men by the ramada looking at her. The man who brought her out was behind her now. He took her nightdress at the neck and pulled down on it. The girl twisted, wrenching away from him, screaming. Some of the men laughed, staring at her now as she tried to hold up her shredded nightdress to cover herself.

The segundo said to Diego Luz, "Maybe we take her

inside and mount her one at a time. Or maybe we do it out here so your family can see."

"I don't know where he is," Diego Luz said.

The segundo looked at Mr. Tanner, who was mounted on a bay horse. The segundo stepped out of his saddle. He took a plug of tobacco and bit off a corner as he walked up to Diego Luz, who watched him, feeling his hands hanging heavily at his sides.

He said to the segundo in Spanish, "Tell him to put my little girl down."

"He's talking," the segundo said.

"Not that one."

"He's a little crazy maybe."

"Tell him to put her down."

"I won't let him do it," the segundo said. "She's too young. Maybe she grow up to be something, like your daughter."

Diego Luz said, "If you touch her you'd better kill me."

"We can do that," the segundo said.

"I don't know where he is. Man, who do you think I put first, him?"

"We only asking you," the segundo said. "Maybe you give us a lot of shit and we believe it. That's a nice-looking girl," he said, looking at the man's daughter. "I like a little more up there, but first one of the day, maybe it's all right."

"Shoot her first," Diego Luz said. "You'd do it to a corpse, you filthy son of a whore."

The segundo said, "Man, hold on to yourself if you can do it. Just tell us."

"I don't know where he is," Diego Luz said.

"Listen, leave Maricopa, you can ride for me."

"I don't know where he is," Diego Luz said.

"I don't care where he is," the segundo said. "I mean it, ride for me."

Diego Luz said, "Come here alone to ask me, I'd try to kill you."

The segundo nodded, smiling. "You'd try it, wouldn't you? That's why I want you."

R. L. Davis came out of his saddle. He walked part way toward Tanner and stopped. He eased his funneled hat up and pulled it down again.

"Mr. Tanner, I'd like to ask him something."

"Go ahead," Tanner said. He brought a cigar out of a vest pocket and bit off the tip.

"I want to ask Diego about seeing him in town with Bob Valdez's clothes three days ago."

Tanner lit his cigar and blew out the smoke. "You hear that?"

Diego Luz nodded his head up and down. "I was taking his clothes to him."

"Where?" Tanner said.

"He was hiding."

"I said where."

"In the line shack. At the Maricopa pasture."

To the segundo Tanner said, "They look in the shack?"

"I'll find out," the segundo said.

"If he wasn't there," Tanner said to Diego Luz, "you're a dead man."

"He brought him his clothes," R. L. Davis said, "and he must've brought him his guns too."

"We've stayed long enough," Tanner said. "Tend to the horsebreaker."

R. L. Davis was standing in the yard. He wanted to say more, but it was passing him by. "Mr. Tanner, I could talk to him some——"

But Tanner wasn't paying any attention to him.

Two men and then a third one brought Diego Luz out in the yard. They bent his arms behind him, forcing him to his knees and this way got him facedown on the hardpack, spreading his arms, a man sitting on him and a man clamping each of his arms flat to the ground with a boot.

The segundo went to one knee at Diego Luz's head. He worked the tobacco from one side of his mouth to the other with his tongue and spit a brown stream close to Diego Luz. He said, "I believe you; you don't know where he is. But maybe you're lying. Or maybe you lie some other time to us. You understand?"

The American with the bony face and the high boots went down to his knees close to Diego Luz's left hand that was palm-flat on the ground. The man drew his Colt revolver and flipped it, catching it by the barrel, and brought the butt down hard on Diego Luz's hand. The hand clenched to protect itself as Diego Luz screamed and the gun butt came down on the tight white knuckles and Diego Luz screamed again. This way they broke both of the horsebreaker's hands while his family watched from the shade of the ramada.

"I mean it," the segundo said, as Diego Luz lay there after the men holding him had moved away. "You come work for me sometime."

They herded the family into the yard to get them out

of the way while they destroyed the house and burned everything that would burn, beginning inside, pouring kerosene on the beds and the furniture, while outside two mounted men were fixing their ropes to the support posts of the ramada. The flames took the straw blinds covering the windows; the men inside poured out with smoke, and as they cleared the doorway, the mounted men spurred away to bring the mesquite-pole awning down over the front of the house. They burned the ramada and the outbuildings and the corn crib. They pulled his corral apart, scattering the horses, and came back across the yard, gathering and riding out southeast, leaving their dust hanging in the air and the sound of them fading in the early morning sunlight.

They were a good mile from the place, moving single file down the bank of an arroyo, the riders milling in the dry stream bed as they moved one at a time up the other side.

R. L. Davis looked back, squinting at the gray smoke rising in the near distance—not a lot of smoke now; the house would be burned out and most of the smoke was probably coming from the corn crib. He turned in his saddle. Tanner was already up the cutbank, but he saw the segundo still in the dry stream bed, waiting for the file of riders to move up. R. L. Davis walked his horse over to him.

"You see that smoke?"

The segundo looked at R. L. Davis, not at the sky.

"I reckon you can see that smoke a good piece," R. L. Davis said. "We're about a mile. I reckon you could still see it eight, ten miles."

The segundo said, "If he's no farther than that and if he's looking this way."

R. L. Davis grinned. "You see what I mean, huh? I was sure you would, though I wasn't putting much stock in Tanner getting it."

"Be careful," the segundo said. "He'll eat you up."

"I don't mean that insulting. I mean he might want to think about it a while, seeing things I don't see——"

"Hey," the segundo said. He took time to squirt a stream of tobacco to the dry-caked earth. "Why do you think he'd come if he sees the smoke?"

"Because they're friends. He brought him clothes and his guns."

"Would you go? If you saw your friend's place burning?"

"Sure I would."

"No, you wouldn't," the segundo said. "But he might. If he sees it he might."

"It's worth staying to find out," R. L. Davis said.

The segundo nodded. "Worth leaving you and maybe a few more." He started off, reining his horse toward the far bank, then came around to look at Davis again. "Hey," the segundo said, maybe smiling in the shadow of his Sonora hat. "What are you going to do if he comes?"

SEVEN

●

"You don't have to tie me," the Erin woman said. "I'll wait for you; I won't run."

Valdez said nothing. Maybe he had to tie her and maybe he didn't, but a mile from Diego Luz's place now and the smoke gone from the sky an hour, he tied her and left her in the arroyo, marking the place in his mind: willows on the bank and yellow brittlebrush in the dry bed. He left her in deep shade, not speaking or looking at her face.

Though he looked at her over and over as he made his way to Diego Luz's place, picturing her in the darkness of the high meadow, the woman lying with him under the blanket, holding her and feeling her against him and for a long time, after she was asleep, staring up at the cold night sky, at the clouds that moved past the moon.

In the morning the sky was clear, until he saw the smoke in the distance, seven miles northwest, and knew what it was as he saw it. Valdez packed their gear without a word and they moved out, across the meadow and down through the foothills toward the column of smoke. At one point she said to him, "What if they're waiting for you?" And he answered, "We'll see."

They could be waiting or not waiting. Or he could have not seen the smoke. Or he could have continued with the woman southeast and been near the twin peaks by this evening. Or he never could have asked Diego Luz to help him. Or he never could have started this. Or he never could have been born. But he was here and he was pointing northwest instead of southeast because he had no choice. At first he had thought only about Diego Luz and his family. But when there was no sign of Tanner, no dust rising through the field glasses, he began to think of the woman more. When she was still with him when they reached the arroyo, he knew he wanted to keep her and tied her up to make sure of it.

Following the dry stream bed north, Valdez saw the tracks where Tanner's men had crossed; he noticed the prints of several horses leading south. He continued on a short distance before climbing out of the arroyo to move west. This way he circled Diego Luz's place and approached from a thicket beyond the horse pasture, studying the house and yard for some time before he moved into the open.

It might have been a dozen years ago after an Apache raid, the look of the place, the burned-out house and the dog lying in the yard; but there were people here, alive, and a team hitched to a wagon, and that was the difference. They waited for him by the wagon, Diego Luz and his family.

Valdez dismounted. "What did they do to you?"

"What you see," Diego Luz said. He raised his hands in front of him, his hands open, the swollen, discolored fingers apart.

"Did they harm your family?"

"A little. If they did any more I wouldn't be here."

"I'm sorry," Valdez said.

"We're friends. They would have come with or without Mr. R. L. Davis."

"He was with them?"

"He saw me in Lanoria with your clothes. Jesus, my hands hurt."

"Let me look at them."

"No looking today. Get out of here."

"What did they ask you?"

"Where you are. Man, what did you do to them?"

"Enough," Valdez said.

"They want you bad."

"They could have followed me."

"But Mr. Davis brought them here. Listen," Diego Luz said, "if you see him, give him something for me."

"For myself too," Valdez said. "You're going to Lanoria?"

"My son is taking me to get these fixed." He looked at his hands again.

"Will they be all right?"

"How do I know? We'll see. I just need to get one finger working."

"I'll take you," Valdez said.

"Go to hell. No, go where they can't find you," Diego Luz said. "I have my boy and my family."

* * *

R. L. Davis came across the Erin woman because he was hot and tired of riding in the sun.

He had moved south along the arroyo with the three riders who would watch with him. "If he comes he'll come from the southeast," the segundo had said. But after the segundo left, R. L. Davis thought, Who says he'll come in a straight line? He could work around and come from any direction. He told this to the three riders with him and one of them, the bony-faced one who'd picked up the little girl and who'd broken Diego Luz's hands, said sure, it was a waste of time; he'd like to get a shot at this Valdez, but it didn't have to be today; the greaser was in the hills and they'd find him.

That one, God, when he'd picked up the little girl, R. L. Davis wasn't sure he could watch what the man wanted to do. Her being a tiny girl.

After a while he said well, he'd double back and take a swing to the north. The others said they'd get up on the banks and look around and head back pretty soon. Good. He was glad to get away from the bony-faced one, a face like a skeleton face, only with skin.

So R. L. Davis moved back up the arroyo. He wasn't looking for anything in particular; there was nothing out here but the hot sun beating down on him. He saw the willow shade up ahead and the bright yellow blossoms of the brittlebush growing along the cutbank. The shade looked good. He headed for it. And when he found the Erin woman in there, sitting in the brush, tied up, he couldn't believe his eyes.

It was a lot to think about all at once. Valdez was here. Had been here. He'd put the woman here out of the way and gone to see Diego Luz. And if he left her like this, tied hand and foot, with a bandana over her mouth, then he was coming back for her. The woman was looking at him and he had to make up his mind fast.

He could pull her up behind him on the sorrel and deliver her to Tanner and say, "Here you are, Mr. Tanner. What else you need done?"

Or he could wait for Bob Valdez. Throw down on him and bring him in as well as the woman. Or gun him if that's the way Valdez wanted it.

The woman looked good. He'd like to slip the bandana from her mouth and get a close look at her. But he'd better not. There was a little clearing in here and rocks that had come down the cutbank. There was room in here to face him. There was room deeper in the brittlebush for his horse, if the son of a bitch didn't make any noise.

God Almighty, R. L. Davis thought. How about it? Bring them both in.

Once he'd moved the sorrel into the brush, he got his Winchester off the saddle and settled down behind the woman, behind some good rock cover. He saw her twist around to the side to look at him, her eyes looking but not saying anything. Probably scared to death. He motioned her to turn around and put one finger to his mouth. *Shhh.* Don't worry; it won't be long.

Crossing the pasture from Diego Luz's place, Valdez saw the willows in the distance marking the arroyo. There had been some luck with him so far, coming in and going out, though he didn't know Tanner and he wasn't sure if it was luck or not. He didn't know yet how the man thought, if he was intelligent and could anticipate what the other man might do, or if he ran in all directions trusting only to luck. Luck was all right when you had it, but it couldn't be counted on. It worked good and bad, but it worked more good than bad if you knew what you were doing, if you were careful and watched and listened. He shouldn't be here, but he was here, and if the luck or whatever it was continued, he would be in high country again late this afternoon, letting Tanner find him and follow him, but not letting him get too close until the time was right for that.

When he talked to Tanner again it had to be on his own ground, not Tanner's.

The sawed-off Remington was across his lap as he approached the willows and entered the cavern of shade formed by the hanging branches. Holding the Remington, he dismounted and stood still to listen. There was no sound in the trees. He moved along the bank of the arroyo, beyond the thick brush below, to a place where the bank slanted down in deep slashes to the dry bed. He worked his way down carefully. At the bottom, as he entered the brittlebush, he cocked the right barrel of the Remington.

The Erin woman sat where he had placed her. She did not hear him or look this way. The bandana covered the side of her face and pulled her long hair behind her shoulders, which sagged with the weariness of sitting here for nearly an hour. You hold her all night and tie her in the morning, he thought. You make love to her, but you've never said her name. Now she turned her head this way.

He saw the startled expression jump into her eyes. He moved toward her, watching her eyes, wide open; her head moved very slightly to the side and then her eyes moved in that direction. Off to the right of her or behind her. Valdez shifted his gaze to the rocks and deep brush.

He moved forward again, a half step, and a voice he recognized said, "That's far enough!"

"Hey!" Valdez said. "Is that Mr. R. L. Davis?"

"Put down the scattergun and unfasten your belt."

Valdez's gaze shifted slightly. There. He could see the glint of the Winchester barrel in the brush and part of Davis's hat. He was behind an outcropping of rock, looking out past the left side, which meant he would have to expose half of his body to fire from that place. If he's right-handed, Valdez thought. He remembered Davis firing at the Lipan woman across the Maricopa pasture and he said to himself, Yes, he's right-handed.

"You hear me? I said put it down!"

"Why don't you come out?" Valdez said.

The sawed-off Remington was in his right hand, pointed down, but with his finger curled on the trigger. He looked at the brush and the edge of the rock outcropping, judging the distance. He imagined swinging the shotgun up and firing, deciding how high he would have to swing it. You get one time, Valdez thought. No more.

"I'm going to count to three," R. L. Davis said.

"Listen," Valdez called. "Why don't you cut out this game and use your gun if you want to use it? What're you hiding in the bushes for?"

"I'm warning you to put it down!"

"Come on, boy, use the gun. Hey, pretend I'm an Indian woman, you yellow-ass son of a bitch."

There. His shoulder and the rifle barrel sliding higher on the outcropping, more of him in the brush, and Valdez swung up the Remington, squeezing his hand around the narrow neck and seeing the brush fly apart with the explosion.

"Hey, you still there?" He shifted the gun to his left hand and drew the Walker. There was a silence. He glanced at the woman, seeing her eyes on him, and away from her.

"I'm hit!" Davis called out.

"What do you expect?" Valdez said. "You want to play guns."

"I'm *bleeding!*"

"Wipe it off and try again."

Silence.

"Boy, I'm coming in for you. You ready?"

He saw Davis at the edge of the rock again, seeing him more clearly now with part of the brush torn away. Davis came out a little more, his left hand covering his ear and the side of his face.

"Don't shoot. Listen to me, don't."

"The first one was for Diego," Valdez said. "The next one's from me. I owe you something."

"I didn't leave you, did I? I didn't let you die. I could've, but I didn't."

"Pick up your gun."

"Listen, I cut you loose!"

Valdez paused, letting the silence come over the clearing. He heard another sound, far away, off behind him, but his gaze held on Davis.

"Say it again."

"After I pushed you over. That night I come back and cut you loose, didn't I?"

"I didn't see you that night."

"Well, who do you think did it?"

His gaze dropped to the woman, to her eyes looking at him above the bandana. He heard the sound again and knew it was a horse approaching, coming fast up the arroyo.

"I left you my canteen. I can prove it's mine, it's got my initials scratched in the tin part, inside."

Valdez raised his Walker to shut him up and motion him out of the brush. Davis started out, then stopped. He could hear the horse.

"Come on," Valdez hissed.

But Davis hesitated. The sound was louder down the arroyo, rumbling toward them. Davis waited another moment then yelled out, "He's in here!" throwing himself behind the outcropping. "Get him! He's in here!"

Valdez reached the woman and pushed her over. He turned, moving crouched through the brittlebush, at the edge of it now, and stepping out of it as the first rider came at him from thirty yards away, drawing his revolver as he saw Valdez and the barrels of the Remington, then seeing nothing as the ten-bore charge rocked him from the saddle. The second rider was down the arroyo coming fast, low in the saddle and spurring his horse, his handgun already drawn, firing it from the off side of his horse. Valdez raised the Walker. He thumbed the hammer and fired and thumbed and fired and saw the horse buckle and roll, the rider stiff, with his arms outstretched in the air for a split moment, and Valdez shot him twice before he hit the ground. The horse was on its side, pawing with its forelegs, trying to rise. Valdez looked down the arroyo, waiting, then stepped to the horse and shot it through the head. He walked over to the man, whose death's head face looked up at him with sunken mouth and open eyes.

"I hope you're one of them Diego wanted," Valdez said. He turned toward the yellow brittlebush, loading the Remington.

"Where was he?" the segundo asked.

"He must have been in them bushes and fired on them as they come by," the rider said. "I was back a piece, up on the west side looking for his sign. When I heard the gunfire I lit up this way and they was coming out of the draw."

The segundo held up his hand. "Wait. You don't want to tell it so many times." He squinted under his straw hat brim toward Tanner, mounted on his bay, looking down at them in the arroyo.

Tanner saw the two bodies sprawled in the dry bed. He saw the dead horse and the yellow-baked ground stained dark at the horse's head. He saw the segundo and a man standing next to him and a half dozen mounted men and a riderless horse nibbling at the brittlebush. Tanner kicked the bay down the bank to the stream bed. He stared at the dead men, then at the segundo, a stub of a cigar clamped in his jaw.

"This man," the segundo said, "is one of the four we left."

"You left," Tanner said.

"I left. He says they went south looking for a sign of him. Then after a while the piss-ant you hired, something Davis, he come back this way."

"Let him tell it," Tanner said, judging the man next to the segundo as he looked at him.

"Well, as he says we worked south a ways," the rider said. "Davis come back first and we spread out some. Then these two here must have started back. I was down there a mile and a half, two miles"—he pointed south, more at ease now, a thumb hooked in his belt— "when I heard the shots and come on back."

"Where were they?" Tanner said.

"When I come back? They were laying there. He must have been in the bushes and fired on them as they come by. As I got close they was coming up out of the draw and going west."

"Who's they?" Tanner asked him.

"Two men and a woman."

"You saw them good?"

"Well, I was off a ways, but I could see her hair, long hair flying in the wind."

"You're saying it was Mrs. Erin?"

"Yes sir, I'd put my hand on the Book it was."

"You see Valdez?"

"Not his face, but it must have been him. One of these boys here was blowed off by a scatter gun."

"That one," the segundo said. "This one, I don't know, forty-four or forty-five, in the chest twice, close together."

"That's five men he's killed," Tanner said. He drew

on the cigar stub; it was out, and he threw it to the ground. "What about Davis?"

The rider looked up. "I figured he was the other one with them. Once I saw he wasn't around here."

"That's the strange thing," the segundo said. "Why would the man want to take him? He's worth nothing to him."

"Unless he went with him on his own," Tanner said. "Mark him down as another one, a dead man when we catch up with them."

"We'll get him for you," the rider said.

Tanner looked down at him from the bay horse. "Did you fire at them?"

"Yes sir, I got down and laid against the cutbank for support and let go till they was out of range."

"Did you hit anybody?"

"I don't believe so."

"But you might have."

"Yes sir, I might've."

"That range you couldn't tell."

"They was two hundred yards when I opened up."

"You could have hit one though."

"Yes sir."

"You could have hit the woman," Tanner said to him.

"No sir, I wasn't aiming at her. No, I couldn't have hit her. There wasn't any chance I could've. See, I was aiming just at Valdez and he was a good piece from the woman."

Tanner looked at the segundo. "Put him against the bank and shoot him."

The rider said, "Mr. Tanner, there was no chance I could've hit her! I swear to God that's the truth!"

The segundo felt the tobacco in his cheek, rolling it with his tongue as his eyes moved from the rider to Frank Tanner, looking at Tanner now but aware of the mounted men behind him and those up on the bank watching. The segundo said, "We lost five now. We shoot our own, that's six, but the same as Valdez killed him. How many you want to give for this man?"

"As many as it takes," Tanner said.

"Instead of shoot him," the segundo said, "we make him ride point. The first one Valdez sees if he's up there waiting. What do you think of that?"

The rider was watching Tanner. "I'll ride point. Mister, I'll cut his sign, too, and get him for you."

Tanner stared down from his judgment seat on the bay horse. He let the man hang on the edge for a long moment before he said, "All right, this time," saying no more than that, but holding his eyes on the man to let him know how close he had come.

The segundo said to the rider, "Start now, come on." He was aware of the men on the bank, beyond Tanner, moving in their saddles, a man wiping his hand across his mouth and another loosening his hat and putting it on again. They were glad it was over. They had killed men, most of them had, but they didn't want to put this one against the bank and shoot him. That would be the end of it. In a few days they would all be gone.

So that was done. The segundo walked over to Tanner's bay; he touched the horse's withers, feeling the smooth flesh quiver and patting it gently. "We have him now," the segundo said, in a voice only for Tanner. "Yesterday he could take us where he wants with plenty of time. Today he has maybe an hour. He has to run and now he doesn't have no more time."

"Say it," Tanner said.

The segundo's hand remained on the horse, patting the firm flesh. "I was thinking to myself, we got eighteen men here. We got six at Mimbreño. We could send eight or ten back and they could start south with the drive. Then when we finish with him we catch up, maybe lose only two days."

Tanner waited. "You through?"

"I mean we don't need so many," the segundo said, but he knew by the way the man was looking at him his words had been wasted.

"I'm going up the mountain," Tanner said. "You're going up the mountain, and all my men are going up the mountain. My men, segundo. You savvy that?"

"If you say it."

"I say it," Tanner said.

Through the field glasses he watched them come up the slope: small dots that he could not count yet, spread in a line, all of them moving this way, one dot ahead of the others, far in front, the only one that he could identify through the field glasses as a mounted rider.

It wasn't happening the way it was supposed to happen. There was open country behind him and he needed more time, a bigger space between them, if he expected to reach the twin peaks. But they were driving him now, running him and making sure he wasn't going to move around them.

It was late afternoon, three hours and a little more until sunset. Three hours to hold them here—if he could hold them—before he could take his two people and slip out. He lay on the ground with good rock cover in front of him and all along the ridge. Next to him were his guns and Davis's Winchester. Looking at the dots coming up he thought, The Winchester or the Sharps? And said to himself, The Sharps. You know it better. You know what it can do.

Well, he had better let them know. Pretty soon now.

He rolled slightly to look at the Erin woman and R. L. Davis. Gay Erin, he said in his mind. Aloud he said, "Mr. R. L. Davis, I would like you to come over here, please, and go down there about fifty feet. You see where those rocks are?"

Davis stood up awkwardly, his wrists tied to his belt with pieces of rope. His elbows pointed out and he looked as though he was holding his stomach. There was dried blood on the side of his face and in his hair and down the arm of his jacket, which was torn and shredded.

"What do you want me down there for?"

"I want you in front of me," Valdez said. "So I can see you."

"What if they come?"

"They're already coming."

Davis gazed down the slope, squinting. "I don't see nothing."

"Take my word," Valdez said.

"Well listen now, if they start shooting I'm going to be in the line of fire."

"Behind the rocks, you'll be all right."

Davis stood his ground. "You still don't believe me, do you? I can prove it by my canteen."

"I don't have your canteen."

"You had it. It's somewhere."

"And we're here," Valdez said. "Let's talk some other time."

"If I didn't cut you loose, who did?"

"You can walk down or I can throw you down," Valdez said.

He looked toward the woman. Say it, he thought. He said, "Gay Erin. Gay. That's your name? Come over here." He watched Davis moving hunch-shouldered down the slope to the cover of low rocks. He felt the woman near him. As she sank to the ground, he handed her the field glasses. "Count them for me."

He raised up to take Davis's Colt out of his belt. The barrel was cutting into his hip. He placed it on the ground next to him and took the heavy Sharps, the Big Fifty, and laid it on the flat surface of the rock in front of him. He would load from the cartridge belt across his chest. With the stock against his cheek, aware of the oiled metal smell of the gun, he sighted down the barrel. Nothing. Not without the glasses.

"Seventeen," the Erin woman said.

He took the glasses from her. Putting them to his eyes the lower part of the slope came up to him.

They were still far enough away that he could see all of them without sweeping the glasses. He estimated the distance, the first man, the point rider, at six hundred yards, the rest of them at least two hundred yards behind him. The brave one, Valdez thought. Maybe the segundo. Maybe Tanner. He held the glasses on the man until he knew it was not Tanner. Nor the segundo, because of the man's dark hat.

Valdez lowered the glasses. He said, "Nineteen. You missed two of them, but that's very good." He looked at her, at her hair in the afternoon sunlight, the bandana pulled down from her face, loose around her neck now. He reached over and touched the bandana, feeling the cotton cloth between his fingers. "Put this on your head."

"The sun doesn't bother me," she said. She had not spoken since they left the arroyo.

"I'm not thinking of the sun. I'm thinking how far you can see yellow hair."

As she untied the knot behind her neck she said, "You believed I cut you loose. I didn't tell you I did."

"But you let me believe it."

"How do you know he did?"

"Because he told me. Because if someone else did it, he would think I knew who did it and he wouldn't bother to lie. I think I was dreaming of a woman giving me water," Valdez said. "So when I tried to remember what happened, I thought it was a woman."

"I didn't mean to lie to you," she said. "I was afraid."

"I can see it," Valdez said. "If you saved my life, I'm not going to shoot you. Or if you get under a blanket with me."

"I tried to explain how I felt," she said.

"Sure, you're all alone, you need somebody. Don't

worry anymore. I know a place you can work, make a lot of money."

"If you think I'm lying," the woman said, "or if you think I'm a whore, there's nothing I can do about it. Think what you like."

"I've got something else to think about," Valdez said. He studied the slope through the field glasses, past Davis lying behind the rock looking up at him, to the point rider. He raised up then and said to Davis, "If you call out, I give you the first one."

He put the glasses on the point man again, three hundred yards away, and held him in focus until he was less than two hundred yards and he could see the man's face and the way the man was squinting, his gaze inching over the hillside. I don't know you, Valdez said to the man. I have nothing against you. He put down the field glasses and turned the Sharps on the point rider. He could still see the man's face, his eyes looking over the slope, not knowing it was coming. You shouldn't have looked at him, Valdez thought.

Then take another one and show them something. But not Tanner. Anyone else.

Through the field glasses he picked out Tanner almost four hundred yards away and put the glasses down again and placed the front sight of the Sharps on the man next to Tanner, not having seen the man or thinking about him now as a man. He let them come a little more, three hundred and fifty yards, and squeezed the trigger. The sound of the Sharps cracked the stillness, echoing across the slope, and the man, whoever he was, dropped from the saddle. Valdez looked and fired and saw a horse go down with its rider. He fired again and dropped another horse as they wheeled and began to fall back out of range. The Sharps echoed again, but they were moving in confusion and he missed with this shot and the next one. He picked up the Winchester, getting to his knees, and slammed four shots at the point rider, chasing him down the slope, and with the fourth shot the man's horse stumbled, throwing him from the saddle. He fired the Winchester twice again, into the distance, then lowered it, the ringing aftersound of the gunfire in his ears.

"Now think about it," Valdez said to Tanner.

He would think and then he would send a few, well out of range, around behind them. Or he would have some of them try to work their way up the slope without being seen.

Or they would all come again.

As they did a few minutes later, spread out and running their horses up the slope. Valdez used the Sharps again. He hit the first man he aimed at, dumping him out of the saddle, and dropped two horses. Before they had gotten within two hundred yards they were turning and falling back. He looked for the two riders whose horses he had hit. One of them was running, limping down the hill, and the other was pinned beneath his dead animal.

"You'd better move back or work around," Valdez said to Tanner, "before you lose all your horses."

Make him believe you.

He raised the angle of the Sharps and fired. He fired again and saw a horse go down at six hundred yards. They pulled back again.

Now, Valdez thought, get out of here.

They could wait until dark, but that would be too late if Tanner was sending people around. He had to be lucky to win and he had to take chances in order to try his luck.

He could leave R. L. Davis.

But he looked at him down there with his wrists tied to his belt, and for some reason he said to himself, Keep him. Maybe you need him sometime.

He called to Davis, "Come up now. Slowly, along the brush there."

The woman sat on the ground watching him. The woman who was alone and needed someone and wanted to be held and got under the blanket. In this moment before they made their run, Valdez looked at her and said, "What do you want? Tell me."

"I want to get out of here," she said.

"Where? Where do you want to be?"

"I don't know."

"Gay Erin," Valdez said, "think about it and let me know."

Tanner and the men with him had gotten to the ridge and were looking at the ground and back down the slope to where they had been, seeing it as Valdez had seen it. Now they heard the gunfire in the distance, to the south.

They stopped and looked that way, all of them, out across the open, low-rolling country to the hills beyond.

"They caught him," one of them said.

Another one said, "How many shots?"

They listened and in the silence a man said, "I counted five, but it could've been more."

"It was more than five," the first man said. "It was all at once, like they were firing together."

"That's it," a man said. "The four of them got him in their sights and all fired at once to finish him."

The segundo was standing at the place where Valdez had positioned himself belly-down behind the rocks to fire at them. He picked up an empty brass cartridge and looked at it—fifty-caliber big bore, from a Sharps or some kind of buffalo gun. He noticed the .44 cartridges that had been fired from the Winchester. A Sharps and a Winchester, a big eight- or ten-bore shotgun and a revolver; this man was armed and he knew how to use his guns. The segundo counted fourteen empty cartridges on the ground and tallied what the bullets had cost them: two dead on the slope, two wounded, five horses shot. Now seven dead in the grand total and, counting the men without horses, who would have to walk to Mimbreño and come back, twelve men he had wiped from the board, leaving twelve to hunt him and kill him.

He said to Mr. Tanner, "This is where he was, if you want to see how he did it."

Tanner walked over, looking at the ground and down the slope. "He had some luck," Tanner said, "but it's run out."

The segundo said nothing. Maybe the man had luck —there was such a thing as luck—but God in heaven, he knew how to shoot his guns. It would be something to face him, the segundo was thinking. It would be good to talk to him sometime, if this had not happened and if he met the man, to have a drink of mescal with him, or if they were together using their guns against someone else.

How would you like to have him? the segundo thought. Start over and talk to him different. He remembered the way Valdez had stood at the adobe wall as they fired at him, shooting close to his head and between his legs. He remembered the man not moving, not tightening or pleading or saying a word as he watched them fire at him. You should have known then, the segundo said to himself.

Tanner had sent four to circle around behind Valdez on the ridge and close his back door. A half hour after they heard the gunfire in the distance, one of them came back.

The man's horse was lathered with sweat, and he took his hat off to feel the evening breeze on the ridge as he told it.

"We caught them, out in the open. They had miles to go yet before they'd reach cover, and we ran them, hard," the man said. "Then we see one of the horses pull up. We know it must be him and we go right at him, getting into range to start shooting. But he goes flat on the ground, out in the open but right flat, and doesn't give us nothing to shoot at. He opened up at about a hunnert yards, and first one boy went down and then he got the horse of this other boy. The boy run toward him and he cut him clean as he was a-running. So two of us left, we come around. We see Valdez mount up and chase off again for the hills. We decide, one of us will follow them and the other will come back here."

Tanner said, "Did you hit him?"

"No sir, he didn't look to be hit."

"You know where he went?"

"Yes sir, Stewart's out there. He's going to track them and leave a plain enough trail for us to follow."

Tanner looked at the segundo. "Is he any good?"

The segundo shrugged. "Maybe he's finding out."

They moved out, south from the ridge, across the open, rolling country. In the dusk, before the darkness settled over the hills, they came across the man's horse grazing, and a few yards farther on the man lying on his back with his arms flung out. He had been shot through the head.

Ten, the segundo thought, looking down at the man. Nine left.

"Take his guns," Tanner said. "Bring his horse along."

It was over for this day. With the darkness coming they would have to wait until morning. He took out a cigar and bit off the end. Unless they spread out and worked up into the hills tonight. Tanner lighted the cigar, staring up at the dim, shadowed slopes and the dark mass of trees above the rocks.

He said to the segundo, "Come here. I'll tell you what we're going to do."

EIGHT

●

"**C**hrist," R. L. Davis said. "I need more than this to eat." Christ, some bread and peppers and a half cup of stale water. "I didn't have nothing all day."

"Be thankful," Valdez told him.

Davis's saddle was on the ground in front of him, his hands tied to the horn. He was on his stomach and had to hunch his head down to take a bite of the pan bread he was holding. The Erin woman, next to him, held his cup for him when he wanted a sip of water. She listened to them, to their low tones in the darkness, and remained silent.

"I don't even have no blanket," R. L. Davis said. "How'm I going to keep warm?"

"You'll be sweating," Valdez said.

"Sweating, man it gets *cold* up here."

"Not when you're moving."

Davis looked over at him in the darkness, the flat, stiff piece of bread close to his face. "You don't even know where you're going, do you?"

"I know where I want to go," Valdez answered. "That much."

Toward the twin peaks, almost a day's ride from where they were camped now for a few hours, in the high foothills of the Santa Ritas: a dry camp with no fire, no flickering light to give them away if Tanner's men were prowling the hills. They would eat and rest and try to cover a few miles before dawn.

Ten years before, he had camped in these hills with his Apache trackers, following the White Mountain band that had struck Mimbreño and burned the church and killed three men and carried off a woman: renegades, fleeing into Mexico after jumping the reservation at San Carlos, taking what they needed along the way.

Ten years ago, but he remembered the ground well, and the way toward the twin peaks.

Valdez had worked ahead with his trackers and let the cavalry troop try to keep up with them, moving deep into the hills and climbing gradually into rock country, following the trail of the White Mountain band easily, because the band was running, not trying to cover their tracks, and because there were many of them: women and several children in addition to the fifteen or so men in the raiding party. He knew he would catch them, because he could move faster with his trackers and it was only a matter of time. They found cooking pots and jars that had been stolen and now thrown away. They found a lame horse and farther on a White Mountain woman who was sick and had been left behind. They moved on, climbing the slopes and up through the timber until they came out of the trees into a canyon: a gama grass meadow high in the mountains, with an escarpment of rock rising steeply on both sides and narrowing at the far end to a dark, climbing passage that would allow only one man at a time to enter.

The first tracker into the passage was shot from his saddle. They carried him back and dismounted in the meadow to look over the situation.

This was the reason the White Mountain band had made a run for it and had not bothered to cover their tracks. Once they made it through the defile they were safe. One of them could squat up there in the narrows and hold off every U. S. soldier on frontier station, as long as he had shells, giving his people time to run for Mexico. They studied the walls of the canyon and the possible trails around. Yes, a man could climb it maybe, if he had some goat blood in him. But getting up there didn't mean there was a way to get down the other side. On the other hand, to go all the way back down through the rocks and find a trail that led around and brought them out at the right place could take a week if they were lucky. So Valdez and his trackers sat in that meadow and smoked cigarettes and talked and let the White Mountain people run for the border. If they didn't get them this year they'd get them next year.

Valdez could see Tanner's men dismounted in the meadow, looking up at the canyon walls, studying the shadowed crevices and the cliff rose that grew along the rim, way up there against the sky. Anyone want to try it? No thank you, not today. Tanner would send some men to scout a trail that led around. But before he ever heard from them again, after a day or two in the meadow, seeing the bats flicking and screeching around the canyon's wall at night, he'd come to the end of his patience and holler up through the narrow defile, "All right, let's talk!"

That was the way Bob Valdez had pictured it taking place: leading Tanner with plenty of time and setting it up to make the deal. "Give me the money for the Lipan woman or you don't get your woman back."

He had almost forgotten the Lipan woman. He couldn't picture her face now. It wasn't a face to remember, but now the woman had no face at all. She was somewhere, sitting in a hut eating corn or *atole*, feeling the child inside her and not knowing this was happening outside in the night. He would say to Tanner, "You see how it is? The woman doesn't have a man, so she needs money. You have money, but you don't have a woman. All right, you pay for the man and you get your woman."

It seemed simple because in the beginning it was simple, with the Lipan woman sitting at her husband's grave. But now there was more to it. The putting him against the wall and tying him to the cross had made it something else. Still, there was no reason to forget the Lipan woman. No matter if she didn't have a face and no matter what she looked like. And no matter if it was not happening the way it was supposed to happen. The trouble now was, Tanner could stop him before he reached the narrow place, before he reached the good position to talk and make a trade.

No, the trouble was more than that. The trouble was also the woman herself, this woman sitting without speaking anymore, the person he would have to trade. He said in his mind, St. Francis, you were a simple man. Make this goddam thing that's going on simple for me.

"You say you know where you're going," R. L. Davis said. "Tell us so we'll all know."

You don't need him, Valdez thought. He said, "If we get there, you see it. If we don't get there, it doesn't matter, does it?"

"Listen, you know how many men he's got?"

"Not so much anymore."

"He's still got enough," R. L. Davis said. "They're going to take you and string you up, if you aren't shot dead before. But either way, it's the end of old Bob Valdez."

"How's your head?"

"It still hurts."

"Close your mouth or I make it hurt worse, all right?"

"I helped you," R. L. Davis said. "You owe me something. I could have left you out there, but being a white man I went back and cut you loose."

"What do you want?" Valdez asked.

"What do you think? I cut you loose, you cut me loose and let me go."

Valdez nodded slowly. "All right. When we leave."

Davis looked at him hard. "You mean it?"

Valdez felt the Erin woman looking at him also. "As you say, I owe it to you."

"It's not some kind of trick?"

"How could it be a trick?"

"I don't know. I just don't trust you."

Valdez shrugged. "If you're free, what difference does it make?"

"You're cooking something up," R. L. Davis said.

"No." Valdez shook his head. "I only want you to do me a favor."

"What's that?"

"Give Mr. Tanner a message from me. Tell him he has to pay the Lipan, but now I'm not sure I give him back his woman."

He felt her staring at him again, but he looked out into the darkness thinking about what he had said, realizing that it was all much simpler in his mind now.

It was two o'clock in the morning when Valdez and the Erin woman moved out leading Davis's bareback sorrel horse. They left Davis tied to his saddle with his own bandana knotted around his mouth. As Valdez tied it behind his head, Davis twisted his neck, pushing out his jaw.

"You gag me I won't be able to yell for help!"

"Very good," Valdez said.

"They might not find me!"

"What's certain in life?" Valdez asked. He got the bandana between Davis's teeth and tightened it, making the knot. "There. When it's light stand up and carry your saddle down the hill. They'll find you."

He would have liked to hit Davis once with his fist. Maybe twice. Two good ones in the mouth. But he'd let it go; he'd cut him fairly good with the Remington. Mr. R. L. Davis was lucky.

Now a little luck of your own, Valdez thought.

They walked the horses through the darkness with

ridges and shadowed rock formations above them, Valdez leading the way and taking his time, moving with the clear sound of the horses on broken rock and stopping to listen in the night silence. Once, in the hours they traveled before dawn, they heard a single gunshot, a thin sound in the distance, somewhere to the east; then an answering shot far behind them. Tanner's men firing at shadows, or locating one another. But they heard no sounds close to them that could have been Tanners riders. Maybe you're having some more luck and you'll get through, Valdez thought. Maybe St. Francis listened and he's making it easier. Hey, Valdez said. Keep Sister Moon behind the clouds so they don't see us. They moved through the night until a faint glow began to wash the sky and the ground shadows became diffused and the shapes of the rock formations and trees were more difficult to see. The moment before dawn when the Apache came through the brush with bear grass in his headband and you didn't see him until he was on you. The time when it was no longer night, but not yet morning. A time to rest, Valdez thought.

They moved into a canyon, between walls that rose steeply and were darkly shadowed with brush. Valdez knew the place and the horses snorted and threw their heads when they smelled the water, the pool of it lying still, undercutting one side of the canyon.

The Erin woman moved around the pool while Valdez stripped off the bridles and saddles to let the horses drink and graze freely. He watched her, looking past the horses, watched her kneel down at the edge of the water and drink from her cupped hands. Valdez took off his hat and slipped the heavy Sharps cartridge belt over his head. A time to rest at dawn, before the day brought whatever it would bring. He moved around the pool toward her.

"Are you hungry?"

She looked up at him, shaking her head, then brushing her hair from her face. "No, not really. Are you?"

"I can wait."

"Are you going to sit down?"

"If you're not going to stand up," Valdez said. He went down next to her, touching her hair, feeling his finger brush her cheek and seeing her eyes on him.

He said, "Gay Erin. That's your name, uh? What was it before?"

"Gay Byrnes."

He took her face gently, his palm covering her chin, and kissed her on the mouth. "Gay Erin. That's a good name. You like it?"

"It's my name because I was married to him."

"What do you want to talk about that for?"

"I don't want to talk about it."

"Then don't. Do you know my name?"

"Valdez."

"Roberto Valdez. How do you like Roberto?"

"I think it's fine."

"Or Bob. Which do you like better?"

"Roberto."

"It's Mexican."

"I know it is."

"Listen, I've been thinking about something."

She waited.

"You heard me tell him I don't know if I'm going to give you back or not."

"I told you before," the Erin woman said. "I don't want to go back."

"That's what you told me." Valdez nodded. "All right, I believe you. Do you know why? Because it's easier if I believe you. If I think about you too much, then I don't have time to think about other things."

"What do you think about me?"

"I think I'd like to live with you and be married to you."

She waited. "We've been together two days."

"And two nights," Valdez said. "How long does it take?" He could see her face more clearly now in the dawn light.

Her eyes did not leave his. "You'd marry me?"

"I think I know you well enough."

"I killed my husband."

"I believe you."

"I've been living with Frank Tanner."

"I know that."

"But you want to marry me."

"I think so, yes."

"Tell me why."

"Listen, I don't like this. I don't feel right, but I don't know what else to say. I believe you because I want to believe you. I say to myself, You want her? I say, Yes. Then I say, What if she's lying? And then I say, God-dam, believe her and don't think anymore. Listen, I couldn't do anything to you. I mean if he says, I won't give you the money, shoot her, you think I'd shoot you?"

She shook her head. "No, I didn't think you would."

"So don't worry about that."

"I never have," the Erin woman said. "I may have been feeling sorry for myself, but I didn't lie down with you just because I wanted to be held."

"Why did you then?"

She hesitated again. "I don't know. I wanted to be with you. I still want to be with you. If I'm in love with you then I'm in love with you. I don't know, I've never loved a man before."

"I've never been married," Valdez said.

She took his hand and brought it up to her face. "I haven't either, really."

"Maybe we can talk about it again. When there's time, uh?"

"I hope so," she said.

Believe that, Valdez thought, and don't think about it. He gave her R. L. Davis's Colt revolver and that sealed it. If she was lying to him she could shoot him in the back. She had already killed one man.

Still, it was easier in his mind now. Much easier.

They found R. L. Davis a little after sunup, a hunched-over figure on the brush slope, dragging a saddle and a thin trail of dust. The two men who found him cut him loose. One of them took the saddle and the other pulled R. L. Davis up behind him and they rode double over to where Mr. Tanner had spent the night. He was alone; all the others were still out on scout.

He looked different. Mr. Tanner had not shaved for two or three days, and the collar of his shirt was dirty and curled up. His moustache looked bigger and his face thinner.

R. L. Davis noticed this, though God Almighty, his back ached from dragging the goddam saddle all over the countryside.

"I wouldn't mind a drink of water from somebody."

The rider who'd brought him in was about to hand him a canteen, but Tanner stopped him.

"Wait'll we're through."

"I haven't had no water since last night."

"You won't die," Tanner said. "Less I see I should kill you."

"Mr. Tanner, look at me. He drew down with that scattergun, like to took my head off."

"Where are they?"

"He let me go about four hours ago and headed south."

"Mrs. Erin was with him?"

"Yes sir."

"How is she?"

"She looks fine to me. I mean I don't think he's mistreated her any."

"God help him," Tanner said. "Did you speak to her?"

"No, he was right there all the time. There wasn't nothing I could say he wouldn't've heard."

"Then she didn't say anything to you."

"No sir. He said something he wanted me to tell you, though."

Tanner waited. "Well, goddam it, go ahead."

"He said, 'Tell him he still has to pay the Indin, but I'm not sure now I'm giving him his woman back.'"

Frank Tanner hit him. He clubbed Davis in the face with his right fist and the man sprawled on his back in the dust.

"I didn't say it—he said it! Them are his words."

"Tell it again."

"I swear it's what he said."

"Tell it!"

"He said you're to pay the Indin, but he wasn't so sure he was going to give you your woman back. Them words exactly."

"Did she say anything?"

"No sir, not a word, the whole time I was there."

"He keep her tied?"

"When she was in the draw, but not when he's around. I mean riding or when he's made camp."

"Why'd he let you go?" Davis hesitated and Tanner said, "I asked you a question."

"Well, I reckon to tell you what he said. There's no other reason I know of."

"God help you if there is," Tanner said.

He was mounting his bay horse, when two riders came in with a string of fresh horses. They had walked all night back to Mimbreño from the place where they had left their dead mounts on the slope.

Tanner looked at R. L. Davis. "Put your saddle on one of them," he said. "I want you present when we run him down."

During the early morning the segundo, whose name was Emilio Avilar but who had been called only segundo for the past six years, found three of his men in the mountain wilderness and signaled them, gathering them in. The men were tired and their horses were worn and needed water. They were ready to head back, and Frank Almighty Tanner could whistle out his ass if he didn't like it. They were paid to drive cattle and freight wagons and shoot *rurales;* they had not signed on to chase a man who'd run off with Tanner's woman. That was his lookout if he couldn't keep her home. After all night in the saddle, it was time to unroll the blankets.

The segundo said, "You think he doesn't want to sleep? Man, he has to stay awake, doesn't he? He got to watch the woman, he got to watch for us. Man, ask him what it's like to be tired."

Two of the riders were American and one Mexican, the Mexican a young man who had been hired only a few months before by the segundo.

One of the Americans said it was none of their business. And the segundo said maybe not, but look, the sooner they caught this crazy man the sooner they could ride to Mexico and have a good time.

"You want some fresh water, uh?" the segundo said. "Don't you think he want some fresh water?"

"If he know where it was," one of the Americans said.

"Listen, when are you going to understand what kind of man he is?" the segundo said. "Sure he's crazy, but he knows what he's doing. You think he come down this way if he don't know there's water? Where it is? He's not that crazy."

"Well, him knowing doesn't help us," the other American said.

The segundo took his hat off and wiped his forehead

with his sleeve and set the Sonora hat over his eyes again. He shook his head and said to the man, "Where do I get people like you? You think I work around here six years I don't know where the goddam water is? What kind of segundo doesn't know where the water is?"

"Well, let's go get it," the rider said.

Emilio Avilar, the segundo, smiled. "Sure, I thought that was what you want."

A little later that morning, watering their horses at the pool, the cliffs and sloping canyon walls reflected in the still water, the three riders looked at the segundo and the segundo smiled again. God, there were fresh tracks all over the place close to the bank, two horses and two people: no doubt about it, a man and a woman. They filled their canteens and wiped down their horses and at this moment were willing to follow the segundo anyplace he wanted to go. Hell, let's get him!

"Which way would you go?" the segundo asked.

"Follow their tracks."

"But that take too long," the segundo said. "What if we know where they going?"

"How could you figure that?"

"Two days ago," the segundo said, "he told Señor Tanner to approach the two peaks. You remember?" He lifted his gaze. "We come from a different way now, but there are the two peaks. Why should he change his mind and not go there? The only difference is now he don't have so much time."

The two American riders thought about it and nodded and one of them said, "What's up there?"

The segundo answered, "We find out."

This is all, he thought, watching the three men move out, slouched in their saddles, heads bobbing, sweat staining a column down their spines. No more. He watched them another moment before calling out, "Hey, Tomás!" The riders looked around and the young Mexican he had hired a few months before reined in to wait for him.

In Spanish the segundo said, "You have a ride the other way. Bring Señor Tanner."

The young Mexican picked up his reins, getting ready. "How will I know where to bring him?"

"You'll hear us," the segundo said.

NINE

●

The twin peaks reached above them, beyond the slope that was swept with owl clover and cholla brush, beyond the scrub oak and dark mass of timber, stone pinnacles against the sky, close enough to touch in the clean, clear air.

"Up there," Valdez said. "We go through the trees and come out in a canyon. At the end of the canyon is a little trail that goes up through the rocks and passes between the two peaks and down the other side. You stand in there and look straight up and the peaks look like they're moving in the wind."

The Erin woman's eyes were half closed in the glare; she shielded her eyes with her hand.

"Once we go through there, we see if we can make a slide to block the trail," Valdez said. "Then we don't hurry anymore. We take our time because it takes them a few days to find a way around."

Her gaze lowered and she looked at him now. "A few days. Is that all we'll have?"

"It's up to us," Valdez said. "Or it's up to him. We can go to Mexico. We can go to China if there's a way to go there. Or we can go to Lanoria."

"Where do you want to go?" she asked him.

"To Lanoria."

"He'll come for us."

"If he wants to," Valdez said. "I run today, but not forever. Today is enough."

"Whatever you want to do," the Erin woman said, "I want to do."

Valdez looked at her and wanted to reach over to touch her hair and feel the skin of her sun-darkened cheek and move the tips of his fingers gently over her cracked lips. But he kept his hand in his lap, around the slender neck of the Remington.

He said, "If you want to go back now, you can. I let you go, you're free. Go wherever you want. Tell him you got away from me."

Next to him, sitting in their saddles, their legs almost touching, she said again, "Whatever you want to do."

"We'll go," he said, reaching back and flicking the rope that trailed from his saddle to R. L. Davis's sorrel horse.

They left the trail and started up across the slope on an angle, moving through the owl clover and around the cholla bushes that were like dwarf trees, Valdez leading, aware of the woman behind him, wanting to turn to look at her, but only glancing at her as his gaze swept the hillside and back the way they had come.

Roberto Valdez kept watch up the slope and Bob Valdez, inside him, pictured the woman coming out of an adobe into the front yard: a place like Diego Luz's, alone in the high country, but larger than Diego's, with glass in the windows and a plank front porch beneath the ramada. The woman in a white dress open at the throat and her hair hanging below her shoulders, her hair shining in the sunlight. He would be coming up from the horse pasture and see her and she would raise her arm to wave. God, he would like to ride up to her, twisting out of the saddle, and take hold of her with her arm still raised, his hands moving under her arms and around her and hold her as tightly as a man can hold a woman without injuring her. But he would stop at the pump and have a drink of water and wash himself and then go to the yard, walking his horse, because he would have the rest of his life to do this.

As Bob Valdez pictured this, finally reaching the yard and the woman, Roberto Valdez saw the riders far below them starting across the slope in single file. Six of them and three horses in a string.

Valdez took the field glasses from his saddlebag. He picked out Frank Tanner and R. L. Davis. He saw them looking up this way and saw one of the men pointing, saying something.

Come on, Valdez thought, as they spread apart now and spurred their horses up through the brush. When you get here we'll be gone. But still watching them, counting them again, he thought, If Tanner is here, where is his segundo?

Emilio Avilar watched from above, from the shadowed edge of the timber.

They had the man almost in their sights, Valdez coming across the slope through the scrub oak, leading the horse and the woman behind him, coming at a walk and angling directly toward them, walking into their guns, and now Tanner the Almighty, the white barbarian, had ruined the ambush and was running him again.

God, the man would have been dead in a moment, shot out of his saddle, but now with the woman behind him, kicking their mounts straight up the grade, Valdez had reached the top of the slope and was entering the timber. Not here, where the segundo had waited with his two Americans for almost an hour, but more than a hundred yards away: a last glimpse of Valdez and the woman disappearing into the trees.

The segundo had scouted the timber and the canyon beyond, studying the canyon and the narrow defile at the end of it, and known at once Valdez was coming here. Where else? This man knew the ground and the water sinks and fought like an Apache. Sure Valdez was coming here: to escape through the defile or to stand in it and shoot them one at a time as they came for him.

Don't let him get in the canyon, the segundo had thought. Don't take a chance with him. Wait for him at the canyon mouth and shoot him as he enters. But Valdez would be coming through the cover of the trees and maybe his nose or his ears would tell him something, warn him, and he would run off another way. You have to think of him as you would a mountain lion, the segundo thought. Trap him in the open, away from cover.

So the segundo had gone back through the timber to the edge overlooking the slope and had told his two men very carefully what they would do: how they would watch for him, then study his angle of approach from the cover of the trees, and be waiting for him to walk into it, waiting until he was close to the trees but still in the open, and kill him before he saw them.

But now Valdez was already in the timber. The segundo had told his men to be quiet and keep their horses quiet and listen.

One of them said, "You know he's going for the canyon."

"He reached it, that's all," the other one said. "Once he gets in the hole ain't nobody going in after him."

"Not this child," the first man said. "Tanner can go in himself he wants him so bad."

Christ Jesus, the segundo said to himself. "Will you be quiet!"

They listened.

"I don't hear him," one of them said. "I don't hear a sound."

The segundo drew the two men closer to him, listening, and they listened with him. "Do you know why?" he said. "Because he's not moving, he's listening. He knows we're in here with him."

"He didn't see us."

"When are you going to know him?" the segundo said. "He doesn't have to see you."

"He's got to move sometime," one of them said.

The segundo nodded. "Before Tanner and the others come up. All right, we separate, spread out a little. But all of us move toward the canyon." His voice dropped to a hushed tone. "Very quietly."

* * *

There were open patches where sunlight streaked through the pine branches a hundred feet above, and there were thickets of scrub oak and dense brush. There was an occasional sound close to them, a small scurrying sound in the brush, and there were the shrill faraway cries of unseen birds in the treetops. The birds would stop and in the shadowed forest, high in the Santa Ritas, a silence would settle.

They moved deep into the trees from the open slope before Valdez brought them up to listen. And as he listened he thought, You should have kept going and taken the chance. You don't have time to wait.

He heard the sound through the trees, a twig snapping, then silence. In a moment he heard it again and the sound of movement in dead leaves.

He was right, some of them were already in the trees. But it did no good to be right this time. They should have kept going and not stopped. They weren't going to sneak through and keep running, and now he wondered if the woman should go first or follow him. Follow him through the trees and in the open, if they reached the canyon, then first into the defile while he held them off. He couldn't remember the distance to the canyon. Perhaps fifty yards, a little more. He was certain of the general direction, the way they would point and keep going.

He said to the woman, "The last time we run. Are you ready?"

She nodded once, up and down. Both of her hands were on her saddle horn, but she didn't seem tense or to be holding on.

"I go first," Valdez said. He nodded in the direction.

"That way. You come behind me. Don't go another way around the trees, keep behind me. If you see them in front of us, stay close to me, as close as you can. At the end of the canyon you'll see the opening. You go in first. Don't get off, ride in—it's wide enough—and I'll come in after you."

She nodded again. "All right."

He smiled at her. "Just a little ride, it's over."

She nodded again and tried to smile and now he saw she was afraid.

Valdez dismounted. He untied the sorrel, moving it aside, holding the bridle under the horse's muzzle. As soon as Tanner's men entered the trees he would send the sorrel galloping off and hope they would take off after its sound. He waited, telling Tanner's men to hurry so he would hear them soon; and when it came, moments later, the sound of their horses rushing into the timber, he hissed into the sorrel's ear, yanking the bridle and slapping the Remington hard across the horse's rump as it jumped to a start and ran off through the trees.

"Now," Valdez said.

They were moving, running through the shafts of sunlight and darkness with the beating, breathing sound of the horses and the tree branches cutting at their faces, running through the brush, through the wall of leaves and snapping branches and through a clearing into trees again, now hearing Tanner's men calling out somewhere behind and somewhere off in the timber. Valdez could see the canyon ahead through the foliage, the open mouth of the meadow, the rock escarpment slanting to the sky.

He saw the opening and he saw a rider slash out of the trees in front of him and come around, his horse rearing with the sudden motion. Valdez broke out of the trees straight for the rider, seeing him broadside now and kicking his mount. He bore down on the man, raising the Remington in front of him, and at point-blank range blew the man off the back of his horse.

He was aware of horses behind him and felt the next man before he saw him or heard him coming up on the left. He switched the Remington to that hand, extending it at arm's length, and when he looked, he fired as the rider fired and saw the man go out of his saddle. The man's horse kept running, racing him, and now he felt the wind in the open and saw the sun balanced on the west rim of the escarpment and heard the Erin woman's horse holding close behind him.

A high whine sang through the narrows as a rifle opened up on him. He remembered the sound of gunfire in the canyon from a time before. He remembered the shadowed crevices high on the walls and the thick gama grass. But he remembered the meadow longer than this, a half mile long in his mind. Now it was not half that distance and he was almost to the end.

Another rifle shot sang out as he reached the defile and came around.

The woman would be there, behind him, and ride in and he would follow her.

But the horse that came behind him was riderless.

The horse veered off, seeing the canyon wall. As it moved out of the way, Valdez saw her: she was about thirty yards from him, her horse was down, and she was rising to her feet, holding her head with both hands and looking at the dead horse.

He saw the segundo close beyond her, dismounting and coming up with a rifle in his hands. Valdez wanted to call out to her, "Run! Come on, do it!" But it was too late. The segundo came on, walking through the gama grass with the rifle in his right hand, his finger through the trigger guard. He stopped before reaching the Erin woman.

Valdez loaded the Remington—not thinking about it, but loading it because it was empty and saying to the segundo with his gaze, You want to do something, come on, do it. He was tired, God, at the end of it, but this is what he was saying to the segundo. With the Remington loaded and cocked he walked out to the woman.

She stood with one hand covering the side of her face, dirt and pieces of grass on her dress and in her hair, as she watched Valdez coming. She looked tired and still afraid, her eyes dull and without question or hope.

"Almost, uh?" Valdez said.

"Almost," the Erin woman said.

"Are you all right?" She nodded and he said then, "You don't have to go back with him. Remember that."

A look of awareness came into her eyes, as if she had been suddenly awakened from sleep. "Don't say that."

"It has to be said."

"I go with you. I don't go with him."

"Frank Tanner doesn't know that." Valdez paused. He said then, "Frank," smiling with the weariness etched in his face. "Francisco. Francis. I have a friend named Francis. I don't know what happened to him."

He laughed out loud and saw the startled look come over her and saw the segundo looking at him.

He heard his own laughter again in the canyon and at the far end saw Frank Tanner and men on both sides of him coming out into the meadow. He saw Tanner stop, looking this way.

Gay Erin touched his arm, holding on to it. He said to her, "I don't know why I thought it was funny. This Frank and my friend having the same name. They're not much alike." He smiled, still thinking of it, and watched the segundo approach, the segundo staring at him, trying to understand what would make him laugh.

With his left hand Emilio Avilar raised his hat and wiped his forehead with the same hand and put his hat on again. He said to Valdez. "You have tobacco? For chewing?"

"Cigarette," Valdez said.

The segundo nodded. "All right."

Valdez brought the sack and paper out of his pocket and moved toward the segundo, who stepped forward to meet him. The segundo rolled a cigarette and returned the sack to Valdez, who made one for himself, and the segundo lighted the cigarettes. Valdez stepped back, the cigarette in his mouth, the Remington in his right hand, pointed down.

The segundo said, blowing out smoke and shaking the match, "Tell me something—who you are."

"What difference does it make?" Valdez answered.

He looked beyond the segundo to Tanner coming up with his men spread behind him.

"You hit one yesterday," the segundo said. "I think five hundred yards."

"Six hundred," Valdez said.

"What was it you use?"

"Sharps."

"I thought some goddam buffalo gun. You hunt buffalo?"

"Apache," Valdez said.

"Man, I know it. When?"

"When they were here."

"You leave any alive?"

"Some. In Oklahoma now."

"Goddam, you do it," the segundo said. "You know how many of mine you kill?"

"Twelve," Valdez said.

"You count them."

"You better, uh?" Valdez said.

The segundo drew deeply on the cigarette and exhaled slowly. He was looking at Valdez and thinking, How would you like about four of him? All the rest of them could go home. Four of him and no Tanner and they could drive cattle to Mexico and become rich. And then he was thinking, Who would you rather shoot, him or Tanner? It was too bad the two of them couldn't trade places. Tanner liked to put people against the wall. This one knew how to do it. He didn't need a wall. He could kill a man at six hundred yards, and the son of a bitch kept count.

"It's too bad it turns out like this," the segundo said.

"Well," Valdez shrugged. "It will be settled now. It will be finished."

The segundo continued to study him. "Why don't you give him his woman? Tell him you won't do it again."

"It's not his woman now."

The sergundo smiled. "Like that."

"Sure, it's up to him. He wants her back, he has to take her."

"You think he can't do it?"

Valdez shrugged again. "If he tries, he's dead. Somebody will get me, there are enough of you. But he still will be dead."

"He don't think that way," the segundo said.

Valdez held his gaze. "What do you think?"

"I believe it." The segundo saw Valdez's gaze lift and he moved to the side, looking over his shoulder to see Frank Tanner coming toward them. The segundo backed away several more steps, but Tanner stopped before reaching him. He was holding a Colt revolver at his side. A man behind Tanner took his horse, and the rest of the men, five of them, spread out, moving to both sides, keeping their eyes on Valdez. R. L. Davis was next to Tanner, a few feet to his right.

Tanner was looking at the Erin woman, who had not moved as he approached. He stared at her and his expression showed nothing, but he was making up his mind.

He said finally, "Come over here next to me."

The woman made no move. "I'm all right where I am."

"You better start thinking straight," Tanner said.

"You better have something to tell me when we get home."

"I'm not going home with you."

Tanner took his time. "That's how it is, huh?" His gaze shifted to Valdez. "She better than a Mexican bitch?"

Valdez said nothing.

"If that's how it is, you better tell that whore next to you go get out of the way."

Quietly, Valdez said to her, "Move over a little. Just a little."

Tanner waited. "Have you got something you want to say to me?"

"I've said it," Valdez answered.

Tanner's eyes held on Valdez. He said, "Put this man against the wall over there and shoot him."

He waited and said then, "Emilio!"

"I hear you," the segundo said.

"Take him."

The segundo did not make a move or seem about to speak.

"Number two"—Tanner's voice rose—"I'm telling you something!"

The segundo looked at Tanner now, directly at him. He said, "It's not my woman."

Valdez's eyes shifted to the man, hung there, and returned to Tanner. His hand gripped the Remington lightly, feeling the weight of the gun, the sawed-off barrel hanging at his knee.

Tanner turned his head slowly to the left, to the three men standing off from him, then to the right, to R. L. Davis and the two men beyond him.

"I'm going to give the word," Tanner said.

"Wait a minute!" R. L. Davis said. "I'm no part of this." He saw Tanner looking at him as he edged back a few steps, bumping against his horse and pushing it. "I don't even have a gun."

"I give you mine," the segundo said.

"I don't want one!" Davis was edging back, taking himself out of the group, his eyes holding on the Remington at Valdez's side. "I don't have any fight with him."

In Spanish, the segundo said to the young Mexican on Tanner's left, "Tomás, go home. This isn't yours."

The young man wasn't sure. "I work for him," he said.

"Not anymore. I let you go."

Tanner's head jerked toward the segundo. "What're you telling him?"

"That she's your woman," the segundo said easily. "A man holds his woman or he doesn't. It's up to him, a personal thing between him and the man who took the woman. All these men are thinking, What have we got to do with it?"

"You do what I tell you. That's what you've got to do with it." Tanner glanced both ways and said, "I'm talking to everybody present. Everybody hears me and I'm telling you now to shoot him. Now!"

He looked at his men again, not believing it, seeing them standing watching him, none of them ready to make a move.

"You hear me—I said shoot him!"

Valdez waited in the silence that followed. He waited as Tanner looked at his men, from one to the next. He drew on the cigarette, finishing it, and dropped it and said, "Hey."

As Tanner turned to him, Valdez said, "I got an idea, Frank," and waited another moment. "You have a gun in your hand. Why don't you shoot me?"

Tanner faced him, the Colt revolver at his side. He stared at Valdez and said nothing, eyes sunken in the shadow of his hat brim, dusty and beard stubbled, still looking like he was made of gristle and hard to kill.

But he's not looking at himself, Valdez was thinking, and it isn't an easy thing to raise and fire a Colt at someone. So he jabbed at Tanner saying, "See if your gun is as good as mine. What do you think of something like that? You and I, that's all, uh? What do you need anybody else for?"

Tanner stood stiffly, no part of him moving.

"Let me say it to you this way," Valdez said. "You give me money for the Lipan woman whose husband was killed or you use the gun. One or the other, right now. Make up your mind."

Tanner's hand tightened on the Colt and his thumb lifted to the hammer. He could feel the move he would make and he was looking squarely at Valdez twenty feet away from him, looking at him dead center where the cartridge belt crossed his chest. The moment was there, *now*, but his gaze flickered to the stubby barrel of the Remington and lingered there and the moment was past. His thumb came off the hammer.

"Not today," Tanner said. "Another time."

Valdez shook his head slowly. "No, that was your time. You get one time, mister, to prove who you are."

"I should have killed you three days ago," Tanner said. "I should have killed you, but I let you go."

"No"—the segundo started past him toward the horses, pausing to take the Colt from Tanner's hand—"three days ago you should have started for Mexico."

"Or paid the Lipan woman," Valdez said. "It wouldn't have cost you so much."